Enshrined Evil

A JESSAMY WARD MYSTERY

PENELOPE CRESS, STEVE HIGGS

GW00491882

Contents

Jolly Hockey Sticks

"Would someone get that dog out of here? He's slobbering all over the lace train!" Mum circled around on the floor beneath me, sliding pins into ivory satin. "Jessamy, stand up straight."

I tried to shoo Alfie into the hall from my perch on the kitchen chair. "It's not easy. This chair is wonky."

"Well, so will this hem be if you don't keep still."

Maintaining my balance on the rickety piece of wood was the least of my worries. The legendary Mystic Muriel, local medium and sometime overnight guest at my Aunt Cindy's garden cabin had gone missing.

Muriel, an octogenarian with a direct line to the afterlife, had vanished, literally, into thin air. The last time anyone had seen her was at a seance held in a cottage on the site of the former St. Mildred's Priory in Oysterhaven. Reports claimed that she had successfully channelled a pack of snarling hellhounds before packing up and heading to the pub with a group of young parapsychologists from Stourchester University. I wanted to meet with them soon to see if they could help shine any light on this mystery.

"Mum, perhaps we should do this during the day? The light will be better."

1

My mother huffed from below. "And pray tell me when you have any space in your diary for a fitting. It's just over a week till your wedding day and you have the Bazaar the day after tomorrow, a carol service during the week, midnight mass and services on Christmas Day. Sermons to write. Gifts to distribute. The poor and hungry to feed. All before you walk down the aisle this Saturday. And don't forget the preparations for the Twelfth Night, wassailing in the new year. Or does that not count because it's a nice pagan tradition?"

"Of course, it counts." I snapped.

"Remember, Jessamy, that you, as the Protector of the Triple Wells, will have to lead the procession." Mum wobbled backwards. Her rear end thudded on the tile floor.

"Mum, you shouldn't be crawling around on the stone floor doing this at your age. Let's leave it to the seamstress. Are you hurt?"

She laughed. "Only my pride." Mum rolled to her side, then onto all fours as she tried to steady herself on the seat of the chair I was standing on. Heaving herself upright, she added, "Slip it off, very carefully. Those pins are sharp. I'll put on the kettle."

I did as instructed. My mother was right. It was complete madness planning a wedding day for the twenty-sixth of December when one is the sole vicar in an island parish church. My diary for the next ten days was bursting with important community festivities, on top of my regular round of church-related activities. It was, however, too late to back out now.

Not that I wanted to. I couldn't wait to have Lawrence officially by my side. We had known each other for less than a year, and had only been engaged since the end of October, but why wait? We were both mature enough to know what our hearts desired. In fact, I was never more sure of anything in my life.

I slipped the dress back onto its cushioned hanger and pulled the clear plastic cover down over the shoulders and down to the hem. Then I stretched up to hang it from the door. It was beautiful. Vintage ivory lace ran from the princess cuffs, up the sleeves, and across a scalloped neckline. The satin bodice that sat beneath tapered into a V-shape at the waist. The modestly flared skirt below fanned into a delicate train.

I had opted for the puff sleeves to help disguise my puffier upper arms and preferred ivory, as I felt the cream to be too brash. White was a definite no-no. The lace covered a multitude of sins. I usually have little interest in clothing, but this was very special.

"You know," I walked over to Mum as she poured boiling water into two prepared mugs, "We could take it back to the dressmaker to adjust the hem."

Mum shrugged. "It won't take me a minute to do. The worst part is over. You are such a fidget."

"You wanted me to get rid of the dog." I protested. As if he knew we were talking about him, Alfie nuzzled at my hand. "And he was just hungry." I turned to my furry companion. "Weren't you, boy? Let's sort you out whilst Grandma makes the tea."

"I am not that animal's grandmother. Stupid, clumsy thing." Mum smiled. *She loves him, really.*

I sorted out a bowl of food for Hugo at the same time. Over the short few months Tilly and Alfie had lived in the vicarage, my feline friend had graduated from complete disgust to a begrudging acceptance of his new playmate. I doubted they would ever be best friends, but occasionally, out of the corner of my eye, when he thought I wasn't looking, I would catch exchanges of passing interest, if not full-on affection. Hugo drew the line at sharing the same plate for food consumption, though. Meaning I had to put Alfie's bowl on the floor, whilst Hugo reigned over him with a bowl on the kitchen counter.

Pets fed, I returned to the welcome cup of tea on the oak table. "Mum, you haven't said if you like the dress. You would tell me if you hated it, though, right?"

"Jessie, it's perfect and you will look stunning. I'm just not very good at expressing stuff like that. You know me. Though I would tell you if it was hideous. Which it's not."

"Well, that's a relief." I sighed into my cup. "Lawrence should be here soon. He had a governors' meeting straight after school. The work has been going very well. Most of the children will be out of Portacabins for the start of the new term. It'll be a great way to start the new year."

"I expect 'jolly hockey sticks' will miss her son when he moves in here for good. Few women get to have their sons live at home for half a century."

I wasn't sure if Mum meant that comment as being a good thing. 'Jolly hockey sticks' was her pet name for Lawrence's mother. Disguised as a dig at her athletic English perkiness — Mrs Edwina Pixley had been a member of the British Ladies Olympic Hockey team in the Seventies — this nickname had a barb in its tail. Sometimes my mother could form an instant opinion of someone that was then impossible to shake. Poor Edwina was too sporty for my mother's tastes. I fear she felt a tad threatened.

"Mum, you must stop calling her that. If you could give Mrs Pixley a chance, you will find she is a perfectly lovely woman. You might even become best friends."

Mum placed her mug firmly on the table and straightened herself. "I never said she wasn't a perfectly lovely woman, though what a woman of her age is doing jogging down Back Lane at the crack of dawn each morning, Goddess only knows."

"Mum! She's not a patch on you. You might not run marathons, but you are probably more active. I mean, when are you going to stop running around after me, for example? You need to take it easier too."

"I'm not dead yet, thank you very much." She looked at the clock on the far wall. "Well, I'd best be going. The cart will be here soon. I'll be back in the morning to finish the hem."

"Don't you want to take it with you?" I offered. "It will be quicker on the machine."

"But easier to hand-stitch such delicate material. Don't worry, I'll be out of your hair by elevenses. I have another appointment in town. Susannah is taking me out for lunch."

"Well, I am heading to the mainland in the morning, remember? To talk to those students about Muriel."

"Ah, yes. Muriel's still alive. But, well, you'll find that out tomorrow if you have eyes to see."

4

And with that cryptic sentence hanging in the air, Mum rose, kissed me tenderly on the head, grabbed her hat and coat and made for the door. She had a cart to catch.

A Bridge Game Too Far

I t was my Aunt Cindy who first raised the alarm about Muriel. She and Aunt Pam had arranged to meet Shelta Lee at The Howlet's Wing in Elton to cast spells over some liquorice tea or whatever, and Muriel was a no-show. My aunts were convinced that something supernatural had broken through from the other side. Possibly a spirit who used and abused the portals designed to transport the celestial beings that visit us from time to time.

I had become immune to such talk of goddesses and wells. Whilst my head still struggled to understand it all, I couldn't argue any longer with all the evidence. I used to pride myself on my logic. Yes, I was a woman of the cloth, and technically believed in a higher being, and a host of angels and saints in the heavens. But my faith didn't readily extend to iridescent sibyllic goddesses with a penchant for nonsensical pronouncements. Returning to Wesberrey had changed all that. Now, not only did I know that this parallel world existed, but I also knew and accepted that I would have a role in protecting it.

I had found, though, that the supernatural played a frustrating game of hide and seek with the truth. My visions, or feelings, were patchy, like a weak internet connection on a stormy day. I belong to a generation old enough to remember a time when, as a child, to ensure a good television signal, I would often have to stand alongside the wooden box in the corner of the lounge, holding the internal aerial above my head for hours at a time. Even then, the picture and sound would fade in and out. That was how the psychic messages came through. I would have to be perfectly still and there was no guarantee of receiving anything meaningful, despite my efforts.

The 'Charmed', aka my mother and her two sisters, assured me it came easier with practice, but so far, I was unimpressed with the results.

With Tilly at work and Lawrence due at any moment, I grabbed the opportunity of being alone to silence my mind. If Muriel had passed, I hoped that her spirit would pay me a visit. *Deep breaths in through the nose. Slow and steady.* Nothing. Nada. Zilch.

Muriel must still be alive. But where?

***

From the back of the vicarage garden, a flashlight in the dark announced that Lawrence was on his way home. I hastily hooked the dress off of the door and scooping the train in my arms, ran upstairs to put it back safely in my wardrobe. *The last thing I need is for the groom to see the wedding dress before the big day.*

Alfie and Hugo did a wonderful job of delaying my fiancé in the kitchen, both of them demanding stomachs and ears to be rubbed. I returned to find all three of them on the floor in a playful pile.

"If I didn't know any better, I could believe you come here to visit them, not me."

Lawrence fought his way through the fur. "Don't be silly. Come. Join us."

"I'll pass. I have enough dander on me as it is. Black picks up everything. Mum's only just left, so I haven't had time to cook anything. But I'm sure there's something in the freezer I can nuke, if you are hungry?"

"I can't stay long." Lawrence had righted himself enough to plant a kiss on my cheek. "Mum has some dinner guests over tonight and I promised her not to be late."

"Oh, you should have said. Or maybe you did. I'm sorry. My head is like a sieve at the moment. It won't take me long to change." Lawrence sniffed and shuffled. I could read the guilt on his furrowed brow. "Oh, you didn't say because I'm not invited."

And I'd just been defending Mrs Pixley to my mother!

"Jess, it's not like that. Er... of course you can come." The panic pulsed through Lawrence's eyes. "It's just... I didn't think you would want to. They're Mum's old bridge partners. You know, the head of the girl guides, Ginny Whitaker, and Brown Owl, Mrs Meadows."

"Sounds like a riot." I did my best to look coy. "So, I am invited?"

"I guess it'll be fine. You are going to be my wife in under ten days' time." Lawrence pulled out his mobile phone from his jacket pocket and motioned 'just a minute' with his fingers. "I'll just ring ahead."

I pulled myself up and kissed his bowed forehead. "There's a good boy." Alfie barked his agreement. I patted the clever canine on his furry golden head as I passed. "Good boys all round."

***

Despite being his fiancée, I was an infrequent visitor to his house. Whilst Lawrence was often to be found chomping down on one of my mother's home-cooked meals at the vicarage, I had yet to taste Edwina Pixley's gastronomic fare. That's not to say, my future mother-in-law hadn't made me welcome, but she was not the homely type. The few times I had seen her at home, either she was coming in as I was leaving, or dashing out minutes after I arrived. Lawrence assured me it wasn't personal, that I had passed muster, but inviting me to join their family gatherings was less organic. *Or maybe they didn't have many family gatherings. Just because my family live in each other's pockets...*

"Jess, how wonderful you could join us." Edwina grabbed my coat off me as I stepped over the threshold. "I meant to ask you, well, let's say it crossed my mind. However, in my defence, I thought you would be busy with some church thing or other. And, to be honest, spending an evening with me and my dour old friends, well, I didn't think you would want to waste your time with a bunch of old fossils like us."

"But you invited Lawrence?" I replied pointedly.

"Well, yes. He's my son." She hooked my coat over a vacant wooden knob on the stand in the hallway. "And we needed a fourth." I stared at her blankly. "For bridge. Do you play?"

"Sadly, no. I must be the only vicar in the land that doesn't. Maybe you could teach me?"

"Excellent idea. Righty-o, come along through to the dining room. Everyone else is desperate to get going." Edwina clapped instructions to her son. "Chop, chop, my dear. You shouldn't keep ladies waiting."

The Pixley home was much like its owner - jaunty. Mrs Pixley, as the matriarch, filled each room with playful functionality. Everything had its place. There was a lot of storage. Items and furnishings had to be first practical and then decorative. The character of the house lay in how cleverly it worked. There was no extraneous objet d'art, but every box and jar, every stick of furniture, was colourful and beautifully crafted. Much like Edwina herself, the effect was pleasant, yet also slightly intimidating. I admit, a part of me was terrified of putting a foot wrong — in the house and with my future mother-in-law.

Mrs Pixley led us through to the lounge, where a small games table held centre stage, a green upholstered dining chair positioned on every side. Two of the seats were already occupied. Mary Meadows and her bridge partner and fellow guider, Ginny Whitaker, sat bolt upright like two schoolgirls waiting to be picked for class monitor.

I had met both women before. They were both regulars at mass on a Sunday and, of course, were important women in the parish, given their respective roles as leaders of the local Brownie and Girl Guide packs. Often I would discuss the weather and other typically British titbits of conversation when passing in the church hall, but I had not had the pleasure of getting to know either lady very well.

Barbara, my very faithful and well-informed parish secretary, had advised that Mrs Mead-ows was not a huge fan of female clerics, but was warming to me. I had no similar intel on Ginny Whitaker but was unsurprised to find her and my future mother-in-law firm friends. They both had a formidable air, seemed to have unquenchable sources of energy and a shared passion for Barbour jackets.

"Too many hands now." Mary Meadows protested. "So, which of you is it to be? The headmaster or the reverend?"

"Oh, the headmaster," I assured her. "I have never played. Shocking I know."

I meant that as a joke, but Mrs Meadows shook her head in agreement and seemed to mutter *'women vicars'* under her breath. Barbara was right. Our local Brown Owl didn't give a hoot about me. And, to be honest, I wasn't too keen on Brownies. My parents had forced me to attend a few meetings when I was around seven or eight and I found it all ridiculous. The Cubs learnt woodworking and how to make fires from sticks. Whereas, I prepared for my 'hostess' badge by making a cup of tea and serving it without spilling a drop. The boys went camping, whilst I danced around a plastic owl on a large plastic toadstool, singing a song about being a Sprite. *The sprightly Sprites, Brave and helpful like the knights. Ugh, I still have nightmares!*

At that moment, it occurred to me that for a Christian institution, Brownie ceremonies are steeped in faux pagan rituals. *Pixies, elves, and sprites, Oh My!*

Ginny appeared more sympathetic, though that eye roll when her partner said 'women vicars' may have been in agreement and not the exasperation I took it to be. *Perhaps I should have stayed snuggled up with a good book and a warm cuppa at the vicarage.*

Lawrence, as always, rode in to rescue me. "Jess is here to witness my trumping you both fair and square. As always," he winked.

It's All In The Game

I am sure it is thoroughly thrilling to play bridge, but it's very dull to watch. I kept that opinion to myself, though. The Pixleys were very competitive and took their sport seriously. A chance comment during the summer about how the game of cricket's only attraction was the buffet spread out in the pavilion at half-time had almost ended our relationship.

Lawrence, though not a fan of most outdoor activities because of his allergies, did however share his mother's passion for wasting, I mean, *enjoying* a sunny summer's afternoon watching grown men stand around for hours on a village green. I suppose the lack of running about suited my beau's meagre athletic prowess, though I admit he looked cute in a white cable sweater.

The first rubber went to Ginny and Mary. My future mother-in-law was less than amused and suggested to Lawrence that if he was going to be as useful as a chocolate teapot all night, then he might as well put an actual pot on to brew. This was my moment to score some points of my own.

"I'll get supper ready. You said you'd put some fresh sandwiches in the fridge."

"Jessamy, how kind of you to offer." Mrs Pixley waved me in the kitchen's direction. Collecting up the cards into a pile, she passed them across the table. "Deal the next game, Ginny. Don't be a slouch."

Their kitchen was tiny. It was probably little more than a scullery back in the past, with the main cooking happening on the range nestled in the hearth in the lounge. There was a porcelain sink, some wooden shelves, a small white fridge and an old-fashioned standalone gas cooker with a grill attachment at eye level. In line with the rest of the house, the kitchen was functional.

The only nod to eccentricity were the brass plaques nailed onto the wooden supports around the door. They appeared to show various scenes of rural life. This quaint Victorian cottage kitchen had a cosy charm. In fact, all the current occupants had added was a more efficient layout and some retro-styled modern appliances.

Case in point, the free-standing refrigerator was a powder blue SMEG. *I've always wanted one of them.* I tugged the chrome door handle and pulled out a fine selection of sandwiches, nestled within a charming border of rocket and cherry tomatoes. The kettle was quick to boil, and soon I was returning next door, arms laden with the much-anticipated feast.

I entered the room to hear a chorus of polite cursing. The Pixleys had lost their third game.

"Jessamy, you've saved us from complete annihilation. Mary, dear, let's clear the cards away and have something to eat."

"I'd say three games lost on the trot were a total wipe-out. You just won't admit it." Mary chuckled in response. "We should mark this day in our diaries, Ginny."

The small bridge table opened up to become a reasonably sized dining table. I wondered on what basis they had originally purchased this particular piece of furniture. What came first? The need for a table to eat at or one on which to play. For though it was a fine gaming table, it was a barely functional dining one.

The cards safely stowed away for another night, Edwina relaxed. Her competitive streak turned her into an Amazonian warrior. She took no prisoners, not even her son received any special consideration when the game was afoot. Now, we were chomping down on a pile of cheddar cheese and Branston pickle sandwiches, her demeanour was altogether lighter. "So, my dear, are all the plans in hand for the big day?"

Talk of the wedding soon morphed into the broader conversation of Christmas festivities.

"I hope you aren't planning on making too many changes." Ginny reached across and stabbed an unsuspecting cube of cheddar cheese with the blade of a red Swiss Army knife. "We value our traditions at St. Bridget's, and never more so than at Christmastide. Can't be doing with fancy modern ideas."

Didn't anyone else see that? No? Just me then? Okay. Ignoring the brutal eating behaviour, I pressed on with the conversation. "No, not at all. Apart from the wedding on Boxing Day, everything else will be as before." Not wanting to make a faux pas, or upset a knife wielding community leader, I added, "And, of course, I will expect the Guides to help as usual."

I had no idea what role the Guides and Brownies played in the local yule festivities, but my experience in other parishes had been that they usually have an active part.

"Oh, we will. You can count on our girls." Ginny preened. "Eh, Mary? We'll beat the boys this year."

Mary plucked a cherry tomato from the server and used it to emphasise her point. "Absolutely. They had an unfair advantage last year. What with the Johnson sisters all coming down with chickenpox and then spreading it through the troop like gossip in the mother and toddler group."

"Have no fear, Reverend. Our angel will be atop the parish tree this year in her rightful place come Christmas Eve." Ginny snorted like a pig sniffing out truffles. "Though it has to be said, Brown Owl, that son of yours is crippling our attempts at bringing in fresh blood. You must pull him back into line."

"He's a lost cause, I'm afraid. His father would be most disappointed." Mary removed a crumpled handkerchief from her sleeve and used it to blow away her maternal frustrations. "Jake's father used to run the local Boy's Brigade, you see, Reverend Ward. It was his father's dying wish that our son would take over, but those awful Fisks lured Jake away. And don't talk to me about that Simon Banks. Terrible, terrible man." She turned to Ginny. "I'm not even sure they should leave him alone with young children."

All the names were familiar, but I was struggling to keep up with Mary's accusations. Jake Meadows, her son, was the leader of the Wesberrey Beavers. The Fisks, Francis and Frances (also known as Frank and Fran) ran the local scouts. Fran was Akela for the cubs. *Isn't Akela such a strange term? Taken as it is from Rudyard Kipling's Jungle Book for the mother of the wolf pack.* Her husband, Frank, was in charge of the scouts. Simon Banks was a relative newcomer to the island, possibly bringing with him fancy modern ideas about scouting from the mainland. *Every time I've met him, he's always been completely charming.*

"But the little ones love him." Ginny ripped open a miniature pork pie. "Did you get these from the butcher in Market Square?" She poked at the sausage meat with the knife. "Always reminds me of that boy with the wand."

"Harry Potter?" I ventured.

"Yes, that's your man. It's the specs. Doubt he can see a thing without them." Ginny finished her investigation by tossing the dissected pie in her mouth. "Mind you, his ophthalmic challenges aside, he seems to have caught the eye of young Orla."

Mary choked. "Well, we have to put a stop to that. She's such an innocent, Reverend Ward, our Miss Kerrigan. Comes from a large Irish Catholic family. But we don't hold her religion against her. Do we, Ginny?"

"I should hope not," I responded, with probably a tad too much righteous offence. "I want St. Bridget's to be an open church. And that goes for any organisations that use our parish hall."

Ginny shot her friend a furious look. "Of course, Reverend. 1st Wesberrey Guides and Brownies are open to girls of all faiths and races."

"But only girls." Lawrence pointed out. He had been so quiet that I had almost forgotten he was there.

"Quite right, too." Mary Meadows folded her arms in a defiant huff. "Our members made that decision to offer young women across the globe a safe space to learn and grow. Mixing genders up is not always for the best."

"No." Lawrence straightened himself up, ready to defend his position. "But, I know a lot of the children in my school prefer the beavers because, well, they see it as being more... fun?"

"Fun!"

Ginny placed a comforting hand on her friend's arm. "I think there are many ways to have fun more fitting to young ladies than charging around the parish hall on a Friday night with foam mallets."

Mary looked shocked. "Do they do that?"

"Well, there are a ton of them in their cupboard. What else can they be for? There's too much violence in our society. Don't you agree, Reverend?" *Says the woman waving around a Swiss army knife without a care.*

"Hmm, I think it's part of the human condition. A tendency that many of us have to struggle to resist every day. Like any weakness." I replied.

"Exactly." Mary tapped Ginny's hand in solidarity, "Guiding instils in young women a sense of morals and pride in themselves. It is not about rough-housing and street-brawling but being prepared for all eventualities. Staying calm in the face of adversity and triumphing over all obstacles. Ideally with good penmanship and a steady sewing hand."

"And yet," Edwina joined in, "You actively encourage your girls to go all out against the boys every year with this Christmas feud."

Mary stiffened. "We offer them a healthy challenge. A simple competition that benefits the local community." Taking a decisive sip of tea, she added, "Ginny, I think we should make a move now. Thank you so much for a wonderful supper and an enchanting evening."

"And for letting you win." Edwina smiled.

Both women rose to get their coats. Ginny looked back over her shoulder at their host and grinned. "Whatever helps you to sleep better tonight, dear friend. Same time next week?"

Butt What?

As I had an early start in the morning, and a graveyard of feral cats to nourish before retiring for the night, I took their departure as my cue to thank my future mother-in-law for a lovely evening and set off into the frosty night. Lawrence insisted on walking me home and helping with the evening feed.

"You know, this can be my responsibility after we are married," He said over a mound of tortoiseshell fur.

"We can take it in turns. Tilly is pretty good at lending a hand, but she's got the late shift at the pub tonight."

Tilly had moved into the vicarage whilst she sorted out her father's affairs. The courts had still to determine if her father's house was an asset of the state, because they argued he bought it with money from illegal activities, whereas his lawyer stated Buck purchased it with funds from his more legitimate business activities. With Tilly came Alfie, her former neighbour's golden retriever. Given the trauma of the past few months, both had settled very well in their new home. Lawrence, moving in, in just over a week's time, would complete my little family.

I felt protective over my ward, though legally she was an adult. Tilly had been through more in her short life than many of us experience in a lifetime. She needed a stable home environment, and I was more than happy to provide it. Tilly had plans to go with my nephew, Luke, to university next year, and alongside her job in the Cat and Fiddle was studying an access course online. She needed to complete her ACAS application soon. When she was at home, we would spend evenings eating cheese balls and looking at college prospectuses online. *I will miss her.*

"Jess." Lawrence took my hand as we skidded down the frozen path back to the vicarage. "You know, we've never really discussed how and when I am moving in."

"No, I guess we haven't. I suppose I just presumed as I *actually* have my own home..."

"Well, technically, it belongs to your boss."

"True, but there's no sense in buying a place of our own when the job comes with such splendid accommodation." It hit me I had assumed a lot about our relationship, including Lawrence taking on the role of the Vicar's wife. "But if you would rather we get our own place, I can have a chat with Bishop Marshall. I'm sure we can —"

He swooped in to peck me on the cheek. "Nonsense. We've never discussed it because it's a no-brainer. A bit like that silly dog you have taken on. I'll give him a quick walk before I go."

"You adore Alfie." I kissed him back and tried to run off ahead in a coquettish fashion, but the ground beneath was too slippery. My flirtation ended in humiliation as my feet gave way and my rear landed on a fresh offering from our local cat colony.

Lawrence contained his laughter just long enough to reach out a steadying hand to pull me back up. "Are you hurt?"

"Only my pride." I laughed. Twisting my torso around to survey the damage, I added. "It's good luck, right?"

***

I struggled to lift my bruised behind out of my bed the following morning. *I think I've broken my coccyx.* Tilly was already making breakfast when I crawled into the kitchen.

"Ouch! What happened to you last night? You look terrible."

"Thank you for your kind words. I took a tumble in the graveyard. Just a bit stiff, that's all."

Tilly pulled out a chair and waved me to sit down. "Well, we can't have the bride-to-be hobbling up the aisle now, can we?" I eased myself into place. Pain shot through me as I made contact with the wooden seat. "Can't have you grimacing through the hen night either. I'll go grab a cushion." Tilly floated off into the hallway and returned with some welcome padding. I raised myself up, using the edge of the table for support, as she slid it underneath. "Aren't you going to Oysterhaven today?"

"Yes. I was going to take Cilla to Elton and see if I can pick up some clues about Muriel."

Tilly pulled up a chair beside me. "I'm not sure a scooter is a good idea in your condition."

"My condition? I'm not pregnant." I protested. "A few painkillers and I'll be right as rain."

"You should let Sam take a look before you go making it worse. Shall I call Beverley?"

"No, you don't bring my mother into this, young lady. Haven't you got an online class you should be at?" I reached across the table for the box of cornflakes. *The pain! Maybe I should see Sam before I go?*

Tilly crunched down on a slice of toast. "Not for another hour. I can come with you if you want. Keep an eye on you."

"I'll be fine. Don't fret. Have you hit send on your ACAS form yet?"

"Nope," she smiled. "And don't try to change the subject. Tea or coffee?"

I watched her get up and walk towards the kettle. "Now, who's changing the subject? Coffee. Thank you. I have to go to Elton today. Muriel's been missing for over a week now. No one has seen or heard from her, and well, Cindy is worried sick. And if my Aunt is worried, something must be up."

"Has anyone checked her home? Muriel may be lying there dead. I mean, how old is she?"

The tips of my fingers reached across to the cereal box. "Dave sent a patrol over to her place a few days ago. Nothing."

Tilly noticed my feeble efforts and pushed the packet closer. "Don't any of you have a *feeling* about what may have happened to her? I thought all of you were like tuned-in to these sorts of things." She placed a steaming cup of coffee in front of me, left the milk beside it, and nodded. "For your cornflakes."

"Many thanks. That's just it. When Muriel didn't show up at the shop, my Aunts and Shelta Lee tried some witchy stuff to locate her, but well, they told me it was like there was interference."

"So, what do you hope to find out by going there this morning?"

Good question.

"See if I can pick up on anything they missed. I suppose."

To be honest, I didn't have a clue.

***

I left Tilly to clear away the breakfast things and headed to the bathroom. She was right. There was no way I was going to make it all the way to Elton on my scooter without some form of pain relief. I tracked down an old water bottle and then set about pulling together my very own heated cushion. I knew it wasn't safe to place it unsecured on Cilla's leather seat, so fashioned a stylish workaround by wedging the cushion/hot water bottle in place using a pair of my largest underpants and a pair of tights. Under a heavy coat, I could hide the extra padding. There was no question that my 'bum' looked big in this get-up, but the soothing warmth brought instant relief. I would stop at the Whistle Stop Cafe on the mainland for a pit stop, and that should take me all the way to the other side of Oysterhaven.

Fortunately, I was now a regular visitor at the cafe, and on good terms with the owner. Asking for a refill of hot water was a small ask when I was also paying for a large caramel latte and a trio of glazed mini doughnuts.

I took my time over my freakishly good beverage and watched the world go by from inside their shop window. The double shot, combined with the mug full I had earlier, also helped mitigate the pain. *Caffeine is a wonder drug.*

It was late December; the air outside was beyond chilly. Passersby resembled extinguished dragons - the warmth of their outward breath being a sorry excuse for flames as they steamed up their glasses.

Suitably recharged, inside and out, I climbed back onto Cilla and pootled off toward Shelta Lee's witchy emporium. The last time I visited the Howlet's Wing, Ms Lee had cast a 'High Sense' spell on me, but my awareness of such cunning had increased since then and I was more prepared for her tricky ways. *Though, if she has a potion on her shelves to fix a damaged tailbone...*

The brass bell above the shop door announced my arrival.

"Reverend Ward, welcome back!" Shelta walked around from the back of her counter; arms outstretched for a hug. "I understand you are soon to be wed. Congratulations."

"Thank you. Erm, I don't suppose I could ask a favour, but I need to borrow your kettle."

Return To Howlet's Wing

W ater bottle refilled, I perched myself on a chair in the shop. Shelta offered me a brew made from willow bark. After my last visit, I graciously declined.

"I promise you the only thing you have to fear is a pain-free butt." she chortled. "I won't try to trick you again. Your Aunt Cindy rapped my knuckles over the 'High Sense' spell. Seems you took to it a little too well, from all accounts. But hey, it worked, didn't it?"

I had to concede that it did. "So, what's in this willow bark?"

"It's a very similar chemical compound to aspirin. Are you sure I can't tempt you?"

My coccyx was screaming for me to try anything, no, everything that would help. "You promise it won't make me hallucinate or anything?"

Shelta's lips, shaded in electric blue lipstick, vanished in the broadest of smiles. "I'll put that kettle back on. Now, what do you want to know about Muriel?"

I called out my questions through the door into the anteroom, where she had a makeshift kitchenette. "You were supposed to meet here with Cindy and Pam, right?"

"Yes," Shelta shouted back over the boiling of the kettle. "Muriel is never late, so we got worried pretty early on. I tried phoning her at her house, but there was no reply."

"And did you try to reach out to her in any other way?" I asked.

Shelta popped her head back around the door. "If you mean did we try to talk to her telepathically, well none of us can actually do that. That's high-grade level juju."

I heard a click, the sound of pouring water and then a metal spoon stirring against the sides of a porcelain cup. I grew frustrated not being able to see what Shelta was doing, but as moving off of my chair was a painful proposition I had to tell myself to trust my host.

The door pushed open. Shelta backed out with a mug in each hand. "But we tried to contact her deceased spirit and nothing. Nada. So, we figured she had either forgotten or was resting up after the drama of the night before."

"Right, so you can talk to the dead and not the living?" I sniffed at the woody brew placed before me.

"Well, it's a different plane of existence. Most of us can't communicate with the living like that. Can you imagine the noise? I have no desire to know what mundane thoughts rattle around inside people's heads, do you?"

"No, I guess it would be very tiresome. So, what happened the night before?" I raised the mug to my mouth and sipped cautiously.

Shelta wiggled back in the chair opposite. "You might find it to have a bitter taste. I added some agave nectar. You are all vegans now, right?"

I nodded. *It doesn't taste awful...* "The night before?"

"Yes, well, I know Muriel was working for the local psychic society. They wanted to contact the nun who haunts the cottage at the back of St Mildred's Church."

I choked slightly. "St Mildred's is haunted?" *I think my tongue is going numb.*

"Not the church, the cottage. Legend has it that a pack of rabid dogs hunted a novice, Sister Elizabeth, to death. The hounds belonged to Thomas Cromwell's enforcers. Total thugs, by all accounts. The community at St Mildred's was refusing to accept Henry VIII's dissolution, and several of the sisters went into hiding. Cromwell's men discovered all of them except for Sister Elizabeth. On hearing that her young charge had vanished, the abbess capitulated. And the locals tore the convent walls down. The stones were used to build houses nearby. They did not find her body. Legend goes that her restless spirit remained to prey on other young women."

"Maybe she escaped. I mean, if they never found her?"

"Possibly." Shelta stirred her tea in deep thought. "However, that doesn't explain all the other tales of snarling dogs and women going missing. There have been dozens of unexplained disappearances over the centuries."

"So how come I've never heard of this before? It's quite the tall tale."

"Well," Shelta sighed. "I can't imagine your church being very comfortable circulating stories of nuns dragging innocent young girls to the depths of hell whilst out courting on a Saturday night."

My entire mouth is now feeling strange. "But you know about it," I mumbled.

Shelta grinned. "I'm not your normal churchgoer, now, am I?"

"Do you know who was at the event?" Well, that's what I tried to say. It came out more like 'duh yah nahoo wa af th'vent'.

Amazingly, Shelta understood what I had said. "I suggest you talk to the parapsychology unit at Stourchester University." *Already on my radar.* "And, of course, the Stourchester Psychic Society, and I believe the Spirit Sleuths were there too. They're a local amateur ghost hunters team. I think they have a channel on YouTube." Shelta placed her cup, undrunk, on the countertop. "Don't worry, the numbing effect is only temporary. How's your bottom feeling?"

"Muff bebber." I replied.

***

Back outside, feeling like I had filled my mouth with novocaine, I signed my goodbyes and gently lifted my leg over Cilla's leather seat. Both sets of cheeks were now numb, and as long as I didn't need to talk, I was grateful.

My next destination had to be the haunted cottage. I hoped the willow bark would wear off, from my mouth at least, before I had to speak to anyone else. But hopes are like bubbles. Some float high into the open sky, others explode into a soapy mess before they're even out of the plastic ring. My wish bubble soon burst on the moustache of a certain Inspector Dave Lovington.

"Jess, why am I not surprised to see you here?"

It had been two months since Rosie and I had unmasked Wesberrey's only permanent police presence, PC Taylor, as part of an international human trafficking ring. *The proof if ever there was that you should always watch the quiet ones.* Dave had been away with my other sister, Zuzu, at his family's country estate to visit with his mother and children. This scandalous affair had brought disgrace to the local constabulary and considerable pain to my family. Not only had we all trusted PC Taylor, but we had welcomed his accomplice, and Tilly's father, Buck, into our lives and our hearts.

Truth be told, my taking Tilly into my home wasn't a popular decision, but she had nowhere else to go. In time, I knew they would come around to my way of thinking. It wasn't Tilly's fault; Buck duped her as much as the rest of us. And my nephew, Luke, adored her. When Tilly wasn't working, he was always there, offering the proverbial shoulder to cry on. In time, Rosie and Zuzu would understand it was the Christian thing to do.

Anyway, Zuzu's relationship with the inspector was going from strength to strength and, as for Rosie? She was being whisked off her feet by Bob McGuire. A man who had worshipped her from afar for decades. *See, everything works out in the end.*

"Dave!" *Hurrah, the power of speech has returned.* "Fancy meeting you here."

"I guess you are hunting for Mystic Muriel." he huffed. "I don't suppose my asking nicely that you stay away from my investigation will make any difference?"

I shook my head. "She's an elderly lady. I wouldn't be doing my civic duty if I refrained from offering a helping hand."

"Well," he sighed, "I was just about to take a poke about inside. So, perfect timing. Uncanny, even." Dave lifted a terracotta pot that stood guard by the front door and produced a key.

Soon we stood inside the two-bedroomed stone cottage. Dave explained the owner lived overseas and rented out the cottage on Airbnb. That was how the psychic society had gained access for the seance. That being said, there was little to show that anyone had used it recently apart from some water stains around the sink that hadn't been wiped down fully and a few upturned cups on the draining board. The only unusual feature was one wooden chair turned away from the table.

I ran my fingers along the back. "Do you think this was where they held the seance?"

Dave bowed with all the flourish of an Elizabethan courtier and winked. "Well, you're the one with the psychic abilities. Perhaps you should take a seat and find out."

The thought of sitting in the chair where Muriel had only a few nights before been channelling a mad nun and a pack of hellhounds wasn't the most attractive invitation. "I, er, wouldn't want to mess with police evidence, and er, I'm not too fond of sitting at the moment," I smirked, pointing at the layers of padding on my tush. "Fell over in the graveyard. Far too embarrassing to give you all the details, but let's just say that I will be fine with the wearing something blue, or in this case black and blue, for the wedding."

"Then proceed with caution," he joked.

I hate it when his eyes twinkle like that!

"Fine. But just so you know, I have ingested willow bark. You are lucky my tongue has recovered. I may be too numb to feel anything."

"Well, I won't be allowing you on the premises again, so it's now or never."

Now it is then. I settled myself on the chair with all the gingerness of a cat on a sun-soaked tile. The hot water bottle and cushion provided a soft barrier between me and the hard oak. Within seconds, the now-familiar swirling and nausea took hold.

There were dogs. Loud, slobbering hellhounds crawling around my feet. Screams bounced off the walls. I could make out a series of shadowy figures, huddled together. Then a peachy mist enveloped me. The voices faded. And I sensed I was moving, floating even. The hounds paced back and forth before me like they were leading the way. I felt compelled to follow. When the mist cleared, I was lying on a mound of damp grass. The dogs curled up obediently at my side.

The grass verge I found myself on was at the edge of a pristine lawn. A formal garden wrapped itself around me on all sides. Joy pulsed through me. *Is this what heaven looks like?*

I didn't have time to wonder for long. As I moved to stand, the ground shook around me and the mist returned.

"Jess, are you okay?"

I blinked my eyes open. "Er, yes, yes, I think so."

Dave had crouched down in front of me. "So, is she dead? Did Muriel talk to you?"

"Not sure. I don't think so." I gasped. "She wasn't there. Does that mean she's alive?"

"She wasn't where, Jess?"

"Heaven? She wasn't in heaven."

St Mildred's Cottage

Though limited in intel, the episode in the chair was the only insight the cottage offered. Dave and I searched every crooked nook and dusty cranny, but there was nothing to point to where Muriel had gone.

As we left, I waited for Dave to put the key back under the pot. I tried to act casual, but he saw right through me.

"Uh, uh, uh. I'll be keeping the key for a few more days whilst I complete my investigations." His eye twitched, which I had observed was often a sign of anxiety. "Just in case you, or any of the other ghost seekers, decide to re-enact the other night. The caretaker has a set, should the owner return early."

I had to discover what he knew. "Have you spoken to everyone that was here? I was told there were three groups invited, the psychic society, the Spirit Sleuths and some students from the university."

Dave chuckled. "I don't suppose you are going to tell me who told you this, but your source is very good. I asked them all to come to the station to give statements. So far, I've spoken to everyone present except the Spirit Sleuths. Too busy, they said. However, I've volunteered to go to their lair later this afternoon." He raised his hand. "And before you ask, the answer is no. I don't need an assistant. I let you into the cottage because I thought your gifts might be useful onsite, but I can handle a group of tech nerds by myself. Thank you."

"But you will tell me if you find out anything. We are all worried sick about Muriel, her being a family friend and all."

"Hmm," Dave placed one hand on his hip and used the other to smooth down his moustache. "We'll see. If I think telling you will help me solve the case—"

I clapped my excitement. "Oh, it will. You know it will. Ring me at the vicarage later."

Standing beside Cilla, I watched the inspector get into his police car and drive off. My next stop would be to see Reverend Cattermole. But first, I needed to slip behind the garden wall and remove the now cold water bottle from my trousers. The willow bark seemed to be holding, and I still had the cushion for protection. It was a short walk down to St Mildred's vicarage, and whilst it would be excellent exercise for my battered behind, I didn't like the idea of my bottom sloshing all the way as I walked.

I crouched down to hide my embarrassment, hiked up the back of my coat, reached behind to get the rubber bottle, lost my balance and had to grab a flint stone that jutted out of the wall for support. As soon as my hand met the rock, nausea raced up to my mouth. I teetered for a few moments, trying to get a grip, physically and spiritually. In an instant, I was sitting in a bright fluorescent-lit room, talking to a striking young lady with snazzy acrylic nails. They were hard to miss. I watched her hand conduct every word she spoke. Rolled up on the table in front of her was a voluminous lilac scarf.

If I can find the girl with the scarf, I will find Muriel. I knew she had to be with her.

***

What exactly an octogenarian medium was doing with a young black woman in what looked like a classroom was beyond my grasp. I slumped my back against the wall for a moment to regroup my thoughts. Shelta had said that no one can talk to the living. Only the dead could connect psychically. Did this mean that Muriel was dead, after all?

I stretched my fingers around the jutting rock and closed my eyes again. In an instant I was back in the room and as before, Muriel was in deep conversation with this other lady. A hand floated into the bottom right of my peripheral vision. The angle of the wrist suggested its owner sat next to me — no, behind me? Their thumb was facing left, palm down. *Hold on, it's not coming from behind. This is my hand. I mean Muriel's hand. Except it can't be Muriel's hand! It's too young!*

Though not sporting similar talons to her friend, the hand I saw waving around did not belong to an eighty-year-old. *Maybe I'm not looking through Muriel's eyes.* The hand slipped back out of sight, then returned. Now it held a gel pen. My gaze has turned to a notebook on the table in front of me. I, or rather, whomever I was channelling, was writing something.

- Onions

- Tinned Tomatoes

- Garlic

- Marjoram

What is this? A shopping list or a recipe? At least they have garlic on the list. They can't be vampires.

The stone wall and damp grass were freezing. Not comforting for my already numbed behind. This vision, flashback or whatever it was, could still prove to be a monumental waste of time. However, I was now certain it wasn't Muriel. Perhaps it was one of those other girls who vanished? A shiver ran through my bones. Time to move on. At least at St Mildred's, I will get a warm cup of tea, and probably some cake.

***

Prudence Beckworth, Reverend Cattermole's ageing but incredibly spritely housekeeper and secretary, opened the vicarage door. "Reverend Ward, so wonderful to see you again.

I hear congratulations are in order. Mr Pixley, the schoolmaster, I understand. Quite the catch. Though he's a smite younger than you, I dare say. But these things matter little today, eh?"

"Lovely to see you too, Mrs Beckworth. How's Conrad? Has he found himself a young woman yet to settle down with?"

"I despair of ever having grandchildren and that's a fact." Prudence offered to take my coat. "But there's no rush for the male of the species, I suppose. Whilst there's life, there's hope. Come along to the kitchen. The reverend will be with you soon. His last appointment is running over a bit. Young couple. She found her husband had an online dating app on his phone."

"How awful," I shuffled down the hall behind her. "I imagine Reverend Cattermole is a very good marriage counsellor. He has such a calming manner."

Prudence directed me to a chair and continued about her duties. "That he does, Reverend Ward, that he does."

Fortified by a fresh cup of tea and a doorstop slice of manor house cake, I passed a happy twenty minutes catching up with the latest Oysterhaven gossip. News of Muriel's disappearance was widespread and several rumours were abroad that offered potential solutions. The most popular was that she had left the seance alone and had fallen into a ditch. The roads along her path home are poorly lit. Very easy to slip in the dark. Her body then rolled down a grassy gulley, only to be covered by a mudslide caused by the recent heavy rains.

"Very graphic." I muttered as Prudence offered me seconds. "People have given this a lot of thought."

"Well, it's not every day a local celebrity vanishes like a slice of my cake."

"And, may I say you have excelled yourself this time, Mrs Beckworth. This is delicious."

"I hope you've left some for me." I turned to see Reverend Richard Cattermole hovering in the doorway. "Lovely to see you again, Jess. I thought I heard your voice."

"Yes, sorry to come unannounced, but I was in the area and thought —"

"That you would take the opportunity to ask me to officiate at your upcoming nuptials? I would be honoured."

Heavens! No, Bishop Marshall is conducting the service. What do I say?

"I'm sorry, Richard. You were my first choice, obviously, but Bishop Marshall has already offered and, well, how could I refuse our boss?"

Like one of those inflatable weighted clowns that children hit, Richard rocked back only to bounce straight up, smiling as if nothing had happened. "Not to worry, Jess, old dear. I understand. Good to know I was in the running though, eh?"

I pulled out a chair for him to join us at the table. "Oh, you were more than merely in the running. You were my only choice, but when I asked the bishop for permission, he just assumed —"

"Well, you deserve the best, my dear." He gulped down a large mouthful of cake and then wiped the crumbs that didn't make it off his black shirt. "So, why have you come by this afternoon?"

"I wanted to talk to you about the legend of Sister Elizabeth and the dogs."

Richard rubbed his chubby hands together. I had hit on a subject he was more than happy to regale me with. "You must be referring to the hellhounds. Is this anything to do with Mystic Muriel? I hear no one has seen her since the seance. Wouldn't be the first time someone has gone missing from the cottage."

"Do you know her? Muriel, that is." I asked as Prudence slid another slice of cake onto my plate.

"Of course. Everyone in Oysterhaven knows our local psychic. I guess your aunts knew her better than I did. Our paths rarely crossed. But she was a harmless ole biddy. If she brings people comfort, who am I to judge?"

"I'd only met her a few times. But she seemed compassionate and caring. Genuine, even."

Richard snuffled up the balance of his second slice. "Not sure where I stand on mediums, truth be told. After all, we preach about the afterlife and father, son and holy ghost. Can't really get all judgemental about people who say they can contact the other side. I mean, isn't that what we aim to do with prayer?"

I am always amazed at how accommodating local people are to alternative spirituality. Maybe it's the water around here. Something in the River Stour that makes us all more open-minded. There are many priests I have known in the more metropolitan cities of this fair land that would have far less liberal views towards their local mystics. I guess before I came home to Wesberrey and learnt about my family and my destiny; I was one of them.

Shifting uncomfortably in my seat, I was keen to get the conversation back on track. "So, what can you tell me about the legend, then?"

"Hmm, well, you probably already know that we suspect that the haunting is somehow related to poor Sister Elizabeth, who herself disappeared."

I nodded.

"And she brings with her the hellish hounds that hunted her down on that fateful night. I'll be honest, I have heard dogs howling sometimes, but there are a lot of houses crammed together around here. One family dog can easily set off another. Before you know it, they are all baying like wolves at a moth in one of their cousin's backyards."

Prudence plonked a fresh teapot on the table. "Like that film, you know the one about the dalmatians. They all start each other off, don't they?"

"So what do you make of the tales of young girls going missing?" I asked, my attention flitting from one to the other of my hosts to glean any insights into their real thoughts. I was eager for any clue, any insight that would help piece together this puzzle.

Prudence breathed in deeply. Her eyes looked over my shoulder at the memory beyond. "I've often wondered what happened to Janet Fairbanks. People said she ran off with a merchant seaman. Swedish, they said. Girls did crazy things back then to get away from home. Folks turned the other way. Running away like that was shameful for her family. I just never bought it myself. Janet wasn't the type, you know."

"When was this?"

"Nineteen... sixty six." Prudence swallowed her next thought and sat staring past me. "England had just won the world cup."

"Mrs Beckworth, how old was Janet?"

"Seventeen years, three hundred and sixty-three days. It was her eighteenth that weekend." Her fingers reached up to stop a sniff from her nose. "Anyway, I hope she ran off with that sailor and had a long life eating pickled herring or whatever."

I stretched across the table to take her hand, but Reverend Cattermole beat me to it. "Prudence, you never mentioned this before." Richard turned her hand in his. "Shall we take a moment to pray for her?"

Prudence agreed. We joined hands in a circle around the table, dropped our heads, and closed our eyes. Richard led the prayer. I tried to call out to Janet's spirit. The peachy-pink mist returned, and just like before, I found myself in a garden. This time I sensed I was not alone but couldn't see anyone or anything around me.

"Amen."

"Mrs Beckworth, you must know the date Janet disappeared then. Is there a pattern, perhaps?"

"You mean an anniversary or something? I'm sorry, Reverend Ward, but no. Janet left us in the summer. It's December now." Prudence smoothed her apron down and rose from her chair. "Now, I have to get the dinner on. Will you be staying with us? You are more than welcome. Pork chops tonight. There's plenty to go around. Conrad brought them up fresh from the market this morning."

"No, thank you, I had better head back to the island. Thank you both so much for your generosity. I hope you can both come to my wedding. I would love to see you there. And Conrad too, if he's free."

"Oh, he's free, Reverend Ward. He's always free."

King of the World

Bob McGuire was on evening ferry duty. Bob always seemed to be on duty, or maybe it was just my good fortune that it was nearly always him on shift when I used the service. He hadn't been the skipper on the way out this morning, but I also knew he had plans with my sister first thing, so that wasn't a surprise. Rosie had said that he was taking more time off lately. *Now that the love of his life had noticed him.*

He greeted me with a smile as wide as the harbour mouth. "Vicar! You timed that just right. I think you'll get home before the heavens open." I winced slightly as I dismounted my faithful scooter. "Have you hurt yourself there, Vicar? Can't have you hobbling up the aisle on your big day. You really should be resting as much as possible."

Rosie had given me equally sage advice when I called earlier.

"Have you been talking to my sister? Don't answer that, oh course you have." I laughed. "I slipped over, that's all. Pulled something. I'll be fine by morning. And talking of mornings, I heard that you and Rosie went to the mainland yourselves today."

"Yes, she was kind enough to come with me to buy a suit. Never had reason to have one before."

I scrunched up my face a little. More because the evening sun was setting just above my eye line, but the timing must have suggested to Bob that I couldn't see him dressed up for a special occasion.

"I'm not sure about it either, Vicar, but Rosie said I looked very dapper. Whatever that means."

"I'm sure you will look very handsome. And please, you need to start calling me Jess. Now that you and Rosie are getting more serious." I smiled, but my friendly grin had nothing on the nuclear-powered beam that lit up his face at the thought of dating my sister.

"That I will then, Jess. Feels strange, Vicar, It truly does."

A rose blush flashed across his cheeks as he backed away to cast off. *Is it third time lucky for Rosie?* Teddy was a lying, cheating scumbag, and Buck proved to be even worse. I so wanted my little sister to be happy. She was a Disney princess in my eyes and deserved to find her prince.

There was nothing dashing about Bob. He was a hardworking, honest man. No frills, no driving ambitions. He looked after his sister and her horde of children and ran this ferry with modest pride. He was one of the good guys and had carried a torch for Rosie since school. Some, particularly my older sister, Zuzu, would call him boring. But I saw him as steady and reliable. Rosie saw him as a safe haven. She called him her rock. *He might prefer to be her anchor in troubled seas.*

I walked towards the front of the boat, or rather the bow. The ferry was almost empty. A few straggling commuters huddled for shelter against the channel winds on the covered deck. The salty air whipped at my face, blowing stray hairs into my eyes and mouth and flushing out the last traces of willow bark. The numbness retreated, and the pain took full advantage. My comfy bed beckoned. *I'll give the Walkers' Workout a miss this evening.* What I needed was a long soak in a warm bath.

My thoughts turned to my wedding plans. Shortly I would become Mrs Lawrence Pixley. I had already ordered my new business cards. *Reverend Pixley?* It had a warm and fuzzy feel to it. I would enter my second year at St. Bridget's as a married woman, with a handsome man at my side. Pushing forward to the pointed edge, I punched my arms in the air and called out to the seagulls buffeting ahead. "I'm the king of the world!"

I have no right to be this happy.

***

Back on terra firma, I steadied myself for one more journey to take Cilla back home. Of course, it was Cilla taking me home, and I don't know what I would do without her. Distant memories of long walks around the parish, grabbing horse-drawn taxis to remote hamlets on the outer edges of the island, accompanied me up the hill. *How my life has changed...*

I dismounted in front of the church hall. Raised voices charged at me from within. I unstrapped my helmet and put a speedy finger tousle through my hair to wake it up. If I needed to restore harmony on the other side of the hall door, the last thing I needed was a flat head.

"Cupcakes! No one eats muffins anymore. If we want to win this year, it has to be cupcakes."

"What's the difference? They all come in those paper wrappers. More cost. We need to cut our overheads to get a start on the guides."

"People want wrappers. No one can handle a naked cake these days!"

"What's wrong with a good ole Eccles cake? Eh? They don't need a fancy paper holder."

"No, but you need a trip to the dentist after."

"Especially if Akela makes them, eh, love? Rock cakes are your speciality."

"Doughnuts," I called from the wings. "You should make doughnuts. Ring doughnuts. And use the centres as doughnut bites — two cakes for the price of one."

"Reverend Ward! Sorry, we didn't see you there." A flustered scout leader straightened his woggle.

"I thought I was going to have to break up a fight, Mr Fisk." I joked. "Could hear you arguing from the vicarage."

His wife, Fran, a.k.a. Akela curtsied her embarrassment. "So very, very, sorry Reverend." Her eyes surveyed her feet as she shook her head, "Shameful behaviour. Unbecoming. What must you think of us?"

"I think you are very passionate about baked goods." I tried to catch her eyes so that she could see that I was smiling. "Come now, what is so important as to have you almost at each other's throats?"

Bespectacled junior scoutmaster, Simon Banks, stepped forward to explain. His chest puffed up beneath his khaki shirt. "The cake sale at the Christmas Bazaar. Whichever troop makes the most profit gets to put their figure on top of the parish tree. We won last year." He cast a glance at his colleagues. "And we will do it again this year *if* we bake cupcakes."

Frank Fisk squared off with his younger partner. "But then we need to buy those wrappers. The best way to maximise our profits is to reduce our costs. Wrappers can't be eaten."

"But we can charge more for them. People will pay stupid prices for cupcakes because they are trendy."

Akela wriggled in between the two men. "I like muffins. Why don't we do a selection and let the public decide?"

"No one wants muffins." Both men said at the same time.

"I love a muffin," I interjected, "But everyone loves doughnuts."

"But you need a fryer for doughnuts. We don't have a fryer in the church hall's kitchen. Rules are rules. Members of the troop must make all cakes for the bazaar in the kitchen of the church hall in advance." Fran Fisk mumbled.

"I'm with the Reverend on this," Simon protested. "Everyone loves doughnuts and we don't need fruit or cream, just a fryer. Surely we can get a fryer and put it in the kitchen here. That's not breaking the rules."

Mrs Fisk grew agitated. "Oh, I don't know about that. Health and safety. Those things are dangerous, and I'm not sure we should trust the cubs with boiling oil and batter."

"I will supervise them personally. It will be good for them to learn about kitchen safety."

"Simon, that's a capital idea. And don't forget, Akela, we have Jake as well. I am sure four of us are as able to keep everyone in line." Mr Fisk stepped in to arbitrate.

"Frank, if you are sure? I will have to do a risk assessment and we will need to ensure that the fryer has had a small appliances check before we use it." Fran removed her glasses from the bridge of her nose and rubbed her eyes. "We have a duty of care, you know."

Mr Fisk put a loving arm around his wife. "You care too much, my dear. My little worry-wart. I trust Simon here. He has a way with the boys. They respect him and Jake. Everything will be fine. Just wait and see."

"And please, Mrs Fisk, I promise our star will top that tree again this Christmas. Won't that be wonderful?" Simon preened.

Fran restored her glasses and pulled down firm on her necktie. "Yes, it will be most wonderful indeed."

Friends Reunited

I left the scout leaders to close up and headed back to the relative sanity of the vicarage. Tilly greeted me at the door. "Gotta run, Jess. I walked Alfie. All the cats are fed, and I cooked us some hotpot. Yours is in the oven." She air-kissed me as she bolted past.

"Hotpot? Wonderful. Er, thanks." I called off after her, but her young legs took her out of range before I had finished my sentence.

Lawrence had a P.T.A. meeting that evening, so I knew I would have the whole place to myself all night. *This could be the last time I will have the place totally to myself for a very long time!*

A warm bath and a hotpot dish later, I curled up on the settee to watch *Midsomer Murders*, with a snoring golden retriever pretzeled in front of the fire and an unusually friendly black cat rolled up like a bagel next to my feet.

Soon the men of the house would outnumber me and Tilly, but we could handle them, especially the furry varieties. Married life would be different, though I would be less than a hundred percent honest if I said I wasn't nervous. Every bride has butterflies. It's a monumental life change. I had boyfriends before. I was prone to the occasional crush, but with Lawrence, there was a deep connection I couldn't explain. He made me feel safe, and I was counting down the days until he would make me the happiest woman alive.

The taste of Tilly's hotpot lingered on my tongue. She would soon be off to university, leaving us behind to fend for ourselves. Lawrence and I will starve if we rely on my culinary skills. *Perhaps I should start looking for a housekeeper?*

"What do you think, boys? Should I hire someone to look after us all?"

Both animals twitched their ears to acknowledge my voice but had little else to say on the subject.

"Okay, so let me sound you both out about something more interesting. What do you think has happened to Muriel?" I realised seeking guidance from my pets was an unorthodox approach to solving crime, but needs must. "Perhaps she did fall into a ditch. The poor woman could lie there for months undiscovered. But then she would be dead and I'd be able to talk with her."

Alfie's tail beat up and down. The noxious odour that followed soon explained why.

"Alfie!"

Hugo covered his snout with his paws.

"Very wise, Hugo, it's awful." I turned to the offender. "I think we need to change your dog food, old boy."

Alfie whimpered.

"Don't you pretend it wasn't you! You helped to circulate it!" Guilt followed hot on the tail of the foul smell. A second later, Alfie's nose was nudging my elbow.

I rubbed his head.

"I can't stay angry at you," I said in a silly sing-song voice.

Ear rub delivered to his satisfaction, Alfie returned to his spot, and I returned to my thoughts.

"Who was I, or rather Muriel, talking to? Of course, it might have nothing to do with the missing mystic. Perhaps I was channelling another missing girl? Like Janet Fairbanks?

Except I doubt it was Janet if she went missing decades ago. I don't think they had acrylic nails back in the Sixties."

Hugo's amber eyes stared me down.

"You're right, of course. It couldn't be Janet. But, my furry friend, it does beg the question how many girls have vanished? And if the ghost of Sister Elizabeth and her hounds take young women, why would they be interested in Muriel?"

Why would they indeed?

***

The following morning, though my rear was still feeling sore, I decided against taking a hot water bottle with me all the way to Stourchester.

I left Cilla behind and took the early ferry to the mainland in time to board the commuter train to Stourchester. Though it was busy with half-asleep, suited travellers, I grabbed a window seat in a group of four around a table and made myself comfortable.

I was starting out early because I had arranged to have coffee with Frederico before my visit to the parapsychology unit. *It would be fun to meet up with the crazy Brazilian again.* He said he had some exciting news to share with me. *Intriguing.*

The rhythmic sounds of metal wheels along the rails serenaded my thoughts. Isn't the modern world magical? I organised both meetings via email from my phone as I waited for the ferry yesterday. I had Frederico's address, of course, and located the parapsychology unit's contact details a couple of clicks down on the university's website.

The informative directory also provided intelligence on the members of that unit and their areas of research. Unlike the Psychic Society and the Spirit Sleuths, they were non-believers out to debunk myths and unmask frauds. Could they have had anything to do with Muriel's disappearance? After all, I knew she was the genuine article. Finding a real medium would undo years of research. Would that be enough of a motive to make said medium disappear?

Or perhaps they kidnapped her and are conducting experiments on her in a secret laboratory buried in the bowels of the university?

Jess, listen to yourself! Giving myself an imaginary slap around the face, I pulled out my notebook and jotted down some questions for my meeting later.

As I plotted out my approach, it struck me how keen they had been to meet. My introductory email had merely mentioned that I was a friend of Muriel's and a bit of an amateur detective, and I was hoping they could give me some insight into what may have happened that night. They replied straight away, agreeing to meet. I pulled out my phone to check the message.

Dear Reverend,

Shall we meet tomorrow? I am free from ten o'clock onwards. Ask for me at Reception, and I will come down to meet you.

Yours sincerely,

Tabitha Wells

According to the university's online directory, Tabitha was a doctoral student with a research interest in folklore, myth, and the pseudo-psychology of ancient belief systems. *Sounds fun!*

Tabitha would probably have a very clinical view of the tale of Sister Elizabeth and the hellhounds. It would be interesting to hear her take on what happened that evening, and about the local legend of missing girls.

The train pulled into Stourchester station, and the previously somnolent carriage buzzed with rush hour activity. Briefcases and backpacks jostled for clearance, as their owners squeezed past each other towards the sliding doors. I patiently closed my notebook and placed it back in my handbag. I had a full hour before my first appointment with Zuzu's ex-boyfriend, Frederico.

After following my sister halfway around the world like a tan puppy on an invisible leash, and vowing to never cease in his quest to win back her heart, Frederico had secured a senior role for himself at the university's animal science department. Once installed, despite a flurry of correspondence at the beginning, he had not been in touch with either Zuzu or me for several months.

I hadn't mentioned to my sister that I had plans to meet up with her old flame, not that I suspected she would be terribly interested. My eldest sister was obsessed with the detective inspector. She and Dave had bought a luxurious apartment together overlooking Wesberrey's marina. And, in conversations where I would argue that she had over-shared information about their ongoing relationship, I learnt that their passion remained as strong as ever.

I don't know how they both have the stamina at their age.

Like a lighthouse flare, Frederico's smile greeted me as I turned the corner into the university's refectory. He strode past benches of fawning undergrads to shake my hand. I had forgotten how chiselled his cheekbones were. Though I appreciated Dave's charms, and I had fallen for them myself in the beginning, Frederico's sex appeal was hard to ignore.

"Jessamy, Jessamy, Jessamy! What a pleasure to see my favourite priest again. I have been very, er, what is the word... remiss in my correspondence. Please, may I get you a drink? The coffee here... é tão-assim." He shrugged in disgust. "Mais ou menos. So-so. But excuse me, I have a lecture in an hour. I'm afraid."

I slid into the chair Frederico had pulled out for me. "Not to worry, it's just lovely to see you again. I've been lapse in my correspondence too. I guess we all lead such busy lives these days."

"Yes, this is true. Now, I remember, white americano?"

"Extra hot, please. Thank you."

I ogled his taut backside as he walked to the refectory barista pod on the far side of the hall. *Jessamy, you are soon to be a married woman. A married Anglican vicar at that. Avert your eyes now, you hussy!* Frederico turned and waved from the side of the counter. I giggled like a regency debutante.

Jaunty electronic tones from my mobile brought me back from my lustful thoughts.

Saved by the bell.

It was Inspector Lovington.

"Dave! What a surprise. Are you calling to update me on what you learned from the Spirit Sleuths yesterday?"

"Yes. I must be out of my mind to keep encouraging you with all this. However, the sum of it is that they know very little about what happened to Muriel. I think it's a dead-end, to be honest. I can't see how the psychic evening had anything to do with her disappearance."

I unzipped my bag, took out my notebook, and flipped it open to a clean page. "Tell me what they said. I just need to grab a pen."

I rummaged around the bottom of my handbag whilst Dave spoke. "Well, all they said was that the three groups were there with Muriel, which we already know. They had set up a lot of paranormal equipment, cameras, EMF readers etc. around the house, so they stayed behind to clear down after the rest of them had left. The only thing that piqued my interest, though, was that it was a very active night. They experienced lots of phenomena they can't explain."

I scribbled as fast as I could to catch up with what Dave was saying. "So, did they record anything?"

"They played me sounds of dogs snarling and metal crashing. Lots of banging. I could hear Muriel's voice in the background, though it was hard to make out amidst the screams. It must have been a frightening experience for those who were there. The investigators felt the hounds were pre-recorded. Whilst they couldn't identify the source of the recording, they are convinced it was a hoax."

"A very elaborate one, by the sounds of it." I signalled my gratitude to Frederico as he placed my coffee in front of me. "Dave, thanks for the update. I'm really sorry, but I have to go." Dave said his goodbyes, and I put my phone screen down on the freshly closed notebook.

Frederico's face fell. "You were talking to Inspector Lovington?"

"Yes, I apologise. He called me about a case we are working on."

"Um vencedor digno. He is a worthy champion." Frederico stirred his coffee. "I, too, have found love, Jessamy."

"That's wonderful!" I snorted, coffee pushing through my nasal cavities. I grabbed a paper napkin. "Does she work at the university?"

"She does, indeed. One day, I would love for you to meet her. Her name is also Susannah. Isn't that inacreditável!"

"Yes, it is." *It certainly is.*

Pleased to Meet You, Tabitha Wells

Frederico invited me to watch him in action in the lecture hall, so I sat at the back as close to the door as possible so that I could make quick my escape. His two-hour talk, fascinating though it was learning about the importance of buffy-headed marmosets in seed dispersal to the ecosystem of the Brazilian rainforest, could not keep me from my next appointment.

A flat-iron-faced woman with hair to match called up to the parapsychology department from the Reception desk. "She says to wait over there."

"Thank you," I glanced at her name badge, "Moira."

For a moment 'Moira' appeared confused. She patted her chest, "Oh I'm not Moira, I'm Jan. I borrowed her cardy earlier." Jan pulled the garment open to reveal a second name tag beneath.

"Sorry, *Jan*. But thank you anyway."

"She won't be long." Jan sniffed in reply, then returned her focus to whatever was on her computer screen.

I turned to sit, but the beady receptionist was right — Ms Wells was already strolling to greet me.

"Reverend Ward, I'm so excited to see you. Please follow me." Barely registering my agreement, Tabitha bounced ahead towards the lift. Her slick ponytail flicked back and forth as she walked. The motion was hypnotic.

I guesstimated her age to be mid-to-late twenties, possibly early thirties. She was hard to pin down. Tabitha's face exhibited the serious air of someone several years her senior, and yet her gait was that of a teenager. She slid towards the lift, like Christopher Walken in a Fat Boy Slim video. There was something else that puzzled me. She seemed familiar. *Maybe Ms Wells just has one of those faces?*

Tabitha led me into a glass-walled office on the third floor and pointed at a circular white table edged by four matching plastic bucket chairs.

"Have we met before?" *I had to ask.*

"And how would we have done that?" she replied, looking out of the glass walls down onto the bustling student life beneath.

The room was one of several that faced onto a central atrium. From our vantage point on the uppermost floor, we could see staff and students engaged in a range of studious pursuits. Some were reading alone, others were working on group projects. There was one clearly asleep at his desk, and one couple had pulled down the blinds to their glass box. Their shadows suggested they were very into anatomy.

"Magical, isn't it?" Tabitha continued. "Life, that is. All of us are sharing the same space and time here today, in this building, and yet we are oblivious to each other's existence. Until we reach out and connect. Like I am connecting with you. Maybe our paths have crossed before. Perhaps that is why you think me familiar? But I assure you, Reverend, you have never seen this visage before." She circled a hand around in front of her face. "I, of course, know yours. You have been in the newspaper. Didn't you unmask a murderer recently?"

"Er, several, actually." I shifted in my seat. "Are the other members of the unit joining us?"

Tabitha stiffened. "Yes, yes. Of course. What am I like? I forgot to tell them you were here. I'll just be a few moments."

When they arrived, her companions clearly were there under sufferance. The first to enter was a spectacled young man with close-cropped brown curls. Tabitha introduced him as Ruben, the office geek and the biggest sceptic she had ever met.

Ruben grumbled about this all being a wild goose chase and how he had already given his statement to the police. "My money's on a bizarre publicity stunt to drive up business. I told the inspector that the old lady was obviously in cahoots with the actress who tried to dupe us." He rubbed his left shoulder. "And I still have bruises from charging that door. I should sue the old bag."

Tabitha stroked the sleeve of his denim jacket and coughed. "Reverend Ward knew the old bag, I understand."

"Yeah, Rubes, where's your respect?" The third member of the party sucked through her teeth in disgust. *Now her face is definitely familiar.*

Thanks to my diligent pre-work, I made an informed stab at her name. "LaKeisha, isn't it?" I took a beat to admire her painted nails. "May I say your acrylics are amazing. I'm always intrigued at how you girls work with them being so long."

"She doesn't do any work, that's how." quipped Ruben.

"See, Vicar, this boy has no respect." LaKeisha folded her arms away from Ruben, though her legs twisted closer in his direction.

"Reverend, ignore these two. They need to get a room with a pull-down blind, if you understand my meaning." Tabitha's frustrated smile suggested that such teasing was routine to the point of irritation. "Now, what do you want to ask us?"

I wanted to ask Tabitha if she had plans to make a ragu. I wanted to ask LaKeisha if she had a lilac scarf. Maybe that's why Tabitha felt familiar? I was ninety-nine-point-nine percent sure it was her I had channelled at the cottage and that it was LaKeisha she was talking to.

"Ruben, tell me about this actress you mentioned."

He pushed his glasses back over the bridge of his nose and took a breath. "It was quite a show. Mystic Muriel was very convincing, but she didn't fool me for a second. All the noise. The howling dogs. The shattering wood. Great sound effects. My hat goes off to them, very effective. But it was clearly a tape. They took advantage of the lights going out to swap the medium with the mediocre. A very hammy performance, if you ask me. All that talk of the Jew and the Moor, it was borderline offensive."

I struggled to follow. "You think this actress and Muriel switched places in the blackout?"

"Of course. What other rational explanation is there?" he huffed.

"But that doesn't explain where Muriel is now, though," I muttered mainly to myself, but LaKeisha ventured to answer me.

"Keeping her head down, I shouldn't wonder. When that *actress* took off," LaKeisha used her brightly coloured nails to make bunny ear quotation marks as she spat out the word 'actress'. "She probably took her chance then to slip out the back or something. Or maybe she'd nipped off later when we went to the pub. Either way, she's now probably squirrelled herself away in a bed 'n' breakfast somewhere with her feet up, enjoying a cup of tea and a good laugh at our expense."

"So you saw nothing at all to suggest that anything bad happened to my friend?"

Tabitha smiled and leaned across the white table to take my hand. "I am sure your friend is fit and healthy and enjoying this wonderful gift we call life."

When Tabitha's fingertips reached mine, I felt a nauseous wave wash through me. I wanted to be sick. Physically sick, right there and then. I pulled away. "So sorry, will you excuse me? I'm feeling a little unwell. Is there a toilet nearby?"

Possibly my face was as green as I felt, but I didn't need to ask twice. LaKeisha stood and ushered me out the door. "I need the little girl's room myself. Here, I'll show you where it is."

Covering my mouth with one hand, I waved goodbye to her colleagues and followed LaKeisha to the Ladies'. Once inside the cubicle, I had time to process my thoughts. I wasn't sure what to make of Tabitha. Something was odd about her behaviour. What I knew for sure, with my trousers and knickers around my ankles, was that I no longer felt ill. The feeling of nausea had passed as quickly as it had come on.

Back outside, LaKeisha was drying her hands on a paper towel. I nudged past her to get to the sink. She, in turn, reached across me to drop the crumpled paper into the bin. "She's not been the same since that night, you know."

"Who? Tabitha?" I glanced up at LaKeisha's reflection in the bathroom mirror. She appeared to be biting back her emotions. Her head bobbed up and down. "What do you mean, she's not the same?"

"She was my homegirl, you know what I mean? I never saw myself doing a PhD. I only did psychology because I couldn't think what else to do. My mother just insisted I went to uni, so..." LaKeisha rested her back against the stall. "Anyway, it was Tabs who got me to stay on to post-grad, and well, I've been dealing with people spouting bull all my life. Seems I have a knack for uncovering fraudsters. Parapsychology just fascinates me. Who'd have thought it, right? How are perfectly sane people willing to buy into the deceit? Ruben wants to know how it's done and Tabs, well, she is the most academic of us. Her interest lies in examining how people have explained the supernatural throughout history. And the three of us were like Charlie's Angels, you know?"

I turned off the tap and shook the excess water from my hands. "Aren't they all women?"

"Ruben is an honorary girl." she grinned. "But, like, I mean, since that night, Tabs has become a card-carrying wackadoodle. Now it's all talk of rainbows and unicorns. I miss her cynicism and pragmatism." LaKeisha grabbed another paper towel and dabbed at her lower lashes. "It's probably nothing. Maybe she's been at the magic mushrooms again." She rubbed her fingers together, her nails tapping against each other as she spoke. "That evening freaked us all out. Even Ruben, though he's too macho to admit it. It spooked us real bad."

"So, you're saying her personality has changed?"

"It's subtle, you know. Little things like stopping to dance through the fountain in the main entrance. Like she wasn't even drunk. And that's the other thing. Suddenly she's a wine drinker. Tabs is a beer drinker. The odd lager, especially a San Miguel with a lime slice, but last night she ordered a chardonnay. A freakin' chardonnay!"

"Have you asked her?"

"Yeah, of course. She just says that all this talk of young women going missing. You know, poor old Sister Elizabeth ripped apart by savage dogs and all that. She says she just wants to experience life more. Mix things up."

"Perhaps that's all there is to it." I offered.

LaKeisha blew her nose and shook the doubts out of her head. "Yeah, perhaps. I'd better go back. We have a departmental meeting in a few minutes. There's talk of budget cuts. Don't want to give them any ideas. Can you find your own way out?"

I answered I could and watched as the flustered young woman composed herself in the mirror.

Something had unnerved her. I needed to find out what.

The Last Meeting

S ignalling failure delayed my train back to Oysterhaven, so I popped back to the vicarage for a quick snack before the Parish Council meeting. My unexpected extra travel time, though irritating, gave me an opportunity to reflect on what LaKeisha had talked about in the toilets. I also had time to wonder about the fit of nausea that only happened when Tabitha touched my hand. It was strange. *In fact, everything connected to my mystic friend's disappearance was strange.*

From what I could make out, according to the parapsychology team, Muriel could have disappeared either during the seance or afterwards when they went to the pub. And at some point, she swapped places with an unknown actress. The unknown actress, booked to play the part of Sister Elizabeth, had also vanished — or had she? Dave never mentioned an actress, though Ruben said he had told the police. Does Dave know who she is? Or, perhaps, he doesn't believe there was an actress. Maybe one or both of the other groups was in on it? And if so, is the actress missing or just lying low after her performance? Was Muriel in on it too and is currently sunning herself on the Costa Del Sol?

Which would mean she is still alive! Note to self: ask the inspector about the actress.

I stuffed a slice of buttered toast in my mouth and dashed off to the church hall. It was the last PCC meeting of the year and there was so much left to finalise for Christmas week.

I barged through the door to find Rosemary, Barbara, and Phil, all wrapped up in their winter best, huddled around a calor-gas heater in the middle of the room.

It hit me how much smaller this gathering was than when I first arrived back in January. Of course, poor Rachel Smith had been a member, and we all deeply missed Tom and Ernest.

As if he had read my mind, Phil started the meeting by getting straight to the point. "Right-y-o, first item on the agenda — the appointment of new churchwardens."

A collective shiver went around the group. No one wanted to replace our friends, but the work still needed to be done.

"Has anyone seen Tom or Ernest recently?" I asked.

The trio shook their heads like a well-rehearsed chorus.

The shuffling of winter boots reigned as the only sound before Rosemary raised her gloved hand. "My nomination is for Mary Meadows and her son, Jake. Her husband, Jake's father, used to run the boy's brigade and teach the Sunday School. Mary did too before Reverend Weeks decided it was too old-fashioned."

"I think you'll find he stopped it because no children ever attended." Barbara protested.

"And I said then that was short-sighted." Rosemary huffed. "Lots of young families on the new estate and what with attendance increasing, thanks to the Reverend here, I think we should bring it back."

I squirmed in my chair at the pleasant, but slightly arrogant, thought that I had built up congregation numbers by myself. Though I imagined it had more to do with my crime-fighting celebrity status than my preaching abilities, sadly.

Phil ignored my discomfort and argued on. "And if we do that, then who's going to run the Sunday school? Probably Mrs Meadows, so that would rule 'er out as a warden. 'Owever, I say, let's offer it to the Fisks."

Rosemary crossed her arms tight to her chest. "Not if you don't want world war three. I've already told Mary she could do it."

"Well, you don't have the authority to do that." Barbara hit Phil on the arm, urging him to back her up again.

"I am the treasurer. I have the right." Rosemary replied.

"And I get the final say." I interjected, hoping to stave off any more missiles. The last thing I needed to marshal, a week before my wedding, was a turf battle between the Guide and Scout leaders and their supporters on my parish council. "If either appointment is controversial, perhaps we should look at other candidates?"

"'Ere, 'ere, Vicar. As always, the voice of reason." Phil raised both hands and lowered them slowly in front of the two women on either side. "I say we need fresh blood. Put a notice in the church bulletin and ask for volunteers. Then we can interview them."

"That's an excellent idea, Phil. Okay, Barbara, let's add it to the diary. Though that means we will be without wardens over Christmas week, which means more work for the rest of us."

Rosemary, not one to sit licking her wounds, had a suggestion. "Well, if we can't appoint their leaders as wardens, why don't we ask the scouts and guides themselves to help more? They're at all the services, anyway. As is the school choir. It would be good to get the children more involved. They can help with the hymn books and the collections. Darn sight more useful than baking cakes and making a mess of the kitchen."

Phil and Barbara nodded in agreement.

"Right, that's settled. I'll chat to Lawrence about the choir and will make a point of visiting the guide and scout meetings this week to ask for volunteers. So, Phil, what's next?"

"Well, whilst we're on the subject of cakes. We need to agree on the raffle prizes for the bazaar. I will donate some whiskey from the pub, of course, and Rosemary has been soaking that giant Christmas pud for months."

Rosemary puffed up like a courting pigeon. "Finest Napoleon Brandy."

"Hmm, any non-alcoholic prizes?" I wondered.

Barbara checked through her notebook. "A fifty-pound gift voucher from Bits 'n' Bobs. Free cut and blow-dry at Scissor Sisters. Of course, there's the traditional twenty-pounder from the Bridewell estate—"

My ignorance dripped from my mouth. "Twenty-pounder?"

Barbara looked up. Smirked. Answered "Turkey" and returned to her notes. "Candlelit dinner for two at The Old School House. Free annual ferry pass for a family of four and..." Barbara squinted at the scribble on the page, moving it back and forth as if that action would help decipher the code. "Must be plum duff. Can't remember who offered that, though."

Phil sneaked a glance at his wife's notepad. "Probably from the bakery. Who else would offer a plum duff puddin'?"

"So," I ventured, "We will have a surfeit of winter cakes. Hope I don't win. I have a wedding dress to fit into."

"Always Reverend Weeks's downfall — the bazaar cakes." Barbara covered her mouth as she chuckled to herself. "He would buy them from both the scouts and the guides. To keep their spirits up, he would say. It all depends on who's left in charge when they make them. Mrs Fisk, God bless her, is a terrible cook. They should register her scones as lethal weapons!"

"Yes, but young Simon was over-seeing production last year. He has the touch. Not everyone can bake, Reverend." Rosemary preened. "It's an art form. I say everyone can cook, but it takes a delicacy of spirit to bake. Mrs Fisk hasn't the heart for it."

"They are thinking of doughnuts this year if they can get a fryer." I scanned our small party to see if my comment provoked any objections.

"Well, as long as they perform a thorough risk assessment in advance." Phil pushed his chair back with a screech. "I think doughnuts would go down a treat."

The rest of us shuffled in our seats. I sensed everyone was in desperate need of a refreshing, and warming, cup of tea.

"Right then," I clapped my hands together. "Is the urn on, or should I fill the kettle?"

I walked with Rosemary to the kitchen, whilst Phil and Barbara packed up. "Tell me more about the rivalry between the Guide and Scout Leaders."

Rosemary bustled past me to fetch the tea caddy from the shelf. "Well, Reverend. It's really between the Meadows and the Fisks. Started out as a bit of fun. You know, to add an extra layer of spice to the season, give the children some healthy competition. Mary's late husband, God rest his soul, ran the Boy's Brigade and, well, he didn't have a lot of time for those heathen scouts, as he called them."

I almost choked on my reaction. "Scouts? Heathens!"

"Well, that's John Meadows for you. He was one of those bible-bashing Christians. Could cite you chapter and verse for every occasion. Anyway, over the years, the Scouts stole away the boys from the Brigade. Numbers got so low that John was forced to retire. Not in a position to wreak his own revenge, he encouraged his wife in this feud over the Christmas tree. All very silly, if you ask me. Men!" Rosemary huffed as she plopped four tea bags into the open mouths of the ceramic mugs below.

"And they still play out this competition every year? The most successful bake sale wins the prize of putting their topper on the tree in the church?"

"Yes, it's all a lot of old nonsense. Milk?"

Phil and Barbara crowded in the doorway. A sprig of mistletoe hung from the frame.

"Look!" I directed their gaze upwards.

"Oh, yes. I totally forgot I 'ung this up earlier." Phil leaned down and planted a tender kiss on his wife's surprised lips.

Barbara giggled as her knees gave way, but her charming knight caught her mid wobble. They were like a couple of love-struck teenagers. Watching them embrace warmed my heart more than any cup of tea. Though the warm mug Rosemary placed in my frozen hands was most welcome.

"So, Reverend, this is our last meeting before the big day. No PCC next week because of the carol concert." Our treasurer picked up the remaining mug and lifted it towards her lips. "Do you have everything sorted?"

"I'll be honest. Between Barbara here and my mother, I have had very little to sort. They have arranged everything."

"Well," Phil squeezed Barbara's arm, causing the contents of her mug to spill over the top. "Sorry, my love... I was going to say that the wedding is in good 'ands then."

"It is indeed," I agreed. "One thing I wanted to check quickly before I forget. The concert. It's by candlelight, right? And we have enough candles?"

"Yes." Barbara smiled. "And we have loads of card drip trays in a box in the back cupboard. It's always very popular. That's something else the children could help with. Putting the candles through the holders." She paused. Swallowed her thoughts and looked at Phil. "That used to be Tom and Ernest's job. It would take them hours. Bless them."

Rosemary leaned back against the kitchen countertop. "Rachel helped out, too. She loved Christmas. All the singing and the lights."

I couldn't see if my companions were crying as my own eyes were too full of water to focus on their faces, but I heard the tell-tale sniffs. All of us were missing absent friends.

Time to call in the boss.

I drew my friends together for a group hug.

"Let us pray."

Sisterhood

The next morning, Barbara and I spent an hour working out the logistics for recruiting new churchwardens. We would add a notice to the parish newsletter that week and I would mention it at all the Christmas week services. We decided that a dedicated slot box would sit at the back of the church for people to post their applications, otherwise, there was a risk that some might get lost amongst the Christmas cards and wedding acceptances already filling up the vicarage's wire mail catcher every morning.

The rest of the day presented little out of the ordinary until I met with my sisters for lunch. Business at the Dungeons and Vegans was booming, allowing Rosie to take on staff, which freed her up to manage the online book orders and steal a little time in the day to talk to her favourite sisters.

"So, Lil Sis, how's phase two of your empire shaping up?" I asked, popping a stray shred of beetroot back into my hummus wrap.

Zuzu dipped a carrot baton into a pot of spicy salsa. "Surely, it's phase three? The cafe is one, the gaming room makes two and now the second-hand book thingy is third."

Rosie sniggered into her oat latte. "One, two and three are all going well. Better than I had hoped, to be honest. I run the book club online now. It's like all three businesses collide there in perfect harmony. Luke helped me with the website." Rosie placed her mug on the table and rummaged underneath. "It was Tilly's idea, bless her. People subscribe to a monthly package through the post with the book club's reading suggestion, a selected tea blend, and some vegan baked goodies." She placed some concept boards in front of us. "I am looking into sourcing other treats such as notebooks and other D&V merchandise."

"Tilly's a remarkable young woman. I will really miss her around the vicarage when she moves on. Her spirit is indomitable." I picked up a board. *These ideas are quite brilliant!*

"You have built quite the family for yourself at St. Bridget's. And soon you will be adding in the handsome Lawrence." Zuzu sat back in her chair and clapped excitedly to herald her next statement. "Only you, Jessie, could have the home, the dog, and the kid, even the honeymoon *before* you have sex with the man, or even marry him. It's so Victorian second wife of you. "

"Very *Jane Eyre*." Rosie joined in.

"There's no mad wife in the attic, I promise you." I hid my embarrassment behind a tall glass of apple juice.

"No," Zuzu reached for another carrot. "Only his crazy mother. Don't get me wrong, Jessie, I love Lawrence to pieces. He's perfect for you. But those apron strings will need an axe taking to them."

"Lawrence is a true gentleman and a wonderfully loving son. And he's just as attentive to me. We've talked about the transition. Well..." I realised we hadn't really talked about it much. I assumed he would move in with me at the vicarage. He did too. There wasn't ever really any need for a conversation. We discussed Tilly moving in with us as if it were the most natural thing in the world. I eyed my siblings' continued interest in my pre-nuptial arrangements over the rim of my glass and decided to change the subject. "Zuzu, has Dave mentioned anything to you about an actress?"

"I get it. You don't want to talk about it. But, Jessie, it's important to set out the rules right from the get-go, you know."

"I know. No more bridge nights with Mommie Dearest and friends." My lips curled up, giving away my thoughts on how I would tempt him away from such delights.

"Reverend Jessamy Ward, I see you." Zuzu covered her mouth. Holding onto her most recent mouthful of food as she pointed out my naughty thoughts. "That dog collar doesn't fool me for a second. You are just as big a minx as the rest of us."

"I am looking forward to a very healthy married life." I knew my face was growing as magenta as the neon 'Gaming' sign behind Rosie's head. "Now, back to my question. Has Dave mentioned anything to you about an actress vanishing into the night?"

Zuzu shook her head.

"So, you think there's another disappearance?" Rosie leaned forward. "Another woman gone, just like Muriel?"

"Or with Muriel? I'm not sure."

"Well, Dave hasn't said anything. He interviewed everyone who was there that evening and I think he muttered something last night about handing it over to Missing Persons. There isn't any sign of a crime being committed." Zuzu joined Rosie on the edge of her chair. This latest development intrigued them both.

"Perhaps we can help? I mean, we are always talking about testing our superpowers. Maybe together we can get some more answers."

"Rosie, the Charmed have already tried to contact Muriel. Seems they can only talk to the dead, so they are pretty sure she is still alive."

"But," Zuzu rested her elbows on her knees and joined her hands together. "Remember when we did that thing with the Norma Jean? Perhaps we can do it again. I know where the key is."

Now that revelation piqued my interest. "What, for the cottage?"

"Yeah. He told me to remember where he put it in case he forgot. You know what it's like, you put something in a safe place and then..."

Rosie shuddered. "I'm not sure we should start trespassing and stuff. I mean, I'm all up for a bit of voodoo hoodoo, but that's like illegal, isn't it?"

"That's what makes it exciting. Or... we could rent it out on Air BnB? Then we'd have every right to be there." Zuzu pulled her mobile phone from the handbag by her stilettoed feet. *Heels, in this weather?*

"And you think your man will go for that plan, do you?" I felt such lengths were unnecessary. I also wasn't sure I wanted to spend the night in a haunted house.

Zuzu collapsed back in her chair and crossed her slender legs. *The heels looked good.* "You leave my man to me."

"But when can we do it? I have the shop, and Jess has all the church stuff and the wedding."

Zuzu snapped her fingers. "We'll use it as a base of the hen night. Come on, Oysterhaven has much more to offer for a night out than Wesberrey. If we book the cottage, we won't have to worry about catching the last ferry home."

"You mean, this Saturday? I've already invited a few others along for a meal and a drink. You know, some of my new friends on the island."

"At the Cat and Fiddle? Yes, I forgot. The girls are coming. They're so excited." By girls, my sister meant her three daughters, Phoebe, Clara and Freya, who were coming to stay for my wedding. "Jessie, this is your last chance to let you hair down as a single woman and you want to spend that at the local boozer?" Zuzu was right - it wasn't a very ambitious plan.

"We could go to the pub the parapsychology students went to with Muriel, or the actress, after the seance?"

"Sounds fun!" Zuzu replied in a deadpan tone that conveyed the last thing she thought it sounded like was fun. "Right, the cottage is blocked out for the Saturday night. It's only a two-bed, anyway... But, hey, it's free tomorrow. I say you deserve two hen nights, don't you little sister? Have your party at the Cat and Fiddle with your family and friends, and we'll have a spooky night tomorrow, just the three of us." With a finger flick on her phone screen. "Oops, booked it." Zuzu broke into song. "Sisters are doing it for themselves."

Rosie tried in vain to protest, but Zuzu sang louder as she pulled my younger sister up on her feet to dance along. I remained glued to my seat.

"And the key? What are you going to tell your police inspector lover, eh?" I taunted.

"I will tell Dave I am returning it for him. Kill two birds with one stone. His investigation is over anyway. You know he won't stop me. I just have to time it right." She winked.

Both sisters continued to dance to their own silent disco. They were both so happy. Perhaps we should throw a little caution to the wind. "Okay, I'm in. Lawrence has to go to London for a meeting early the next morning anyway. However, I can't leave until after the Scouts. I need to talk to their leaders about the children volunteering as churchwardens."

Zuzu flung Rosie around. "Can't you email them? Or do it the old-fashioned way and call them?"

"I guess."

Rosie grabbed my hand and yanked it towards her. The rest of my body had no choice but to follow. "That's that then. We are clubbing on the mainland tomorrow. You need to get some dance practice in."

"Annie Lennox eat your heart out. Sisters are doing it for themselves!"

The Rainbow Connection

I might have to dial in my call for Scout volunteers, but the Guides meet on a Thursday afternoon and that is exactly where Cilla and I dashed after lunch. I pulled up alongside the hall and dismounted. This was still a delicate operation. Though my rear end was no longer in as much pain, it was still stiff, especially after bumping up the cobbled streets of Wesberrey.

I lifted my helmet and shook out my hair. There were hushed voices coming from the alleyway at the back. Thinking it was some lost Brownies and Guides messing around, I tiptoed across. There were a couple sporting blue and khaki green uniforms messing around, but they were not lost children.

"Oh, I'm sorry. I thought some of the kids were back here."

Jake Meadows removed his hands from under his companion's blouse and straightened his woggle.

His companion was the pretty Rainbows leader, Orla Kerrigan. As she was Roman Catholic and attended church on the mainland, our paths had seldom crossed. Rainbows' meetings run straight after the school day ends, and I was usually busy elsewhere. I had seen her around, though, helping Mary Meadows with the Brownies, and had always intended to get to know her better. She seemed like a lovely young girl. Now, she was an extremely embarrassed one.

Jake stepped in front of Orla, to protect her honour as she buttoned up her top and readjusted her skirt. "I am so terribly sorry, Reverend. What must you be thinking?" He looked furtively over my shoulder down the alleyway. "My mother's not with you, is she?"

"Jake? How old are you?"

He shifted his body weight from one foot to the other and kicked at something invisible on the ground. "Twenty-one."

I glanced behind him to Orla. "And you?"

Orla's pink freckled face appeared over Jake's shoulder. "Twenty? I'll be twenty-one in February."

"Then, aren't you a tad old to be making out behind the bike sheds?" I smirked.

Jake screwed up his eyebrows, tilted his number two shaved head to his right and said, "But we are behind the church hall?"

Orla stabbed his side with her elbow. "She's not being literal, you idiot."

I raised my hands as a sign of truce and backed away a few steps. "Guys, what I meant was you don't need to sneak around at all. You are both over the age of consent. I think you make a lovely couple."

And they did. Both had a fresh-faced innocence and freckles to match.

Jake hit his clenched fist against the cold air, more in anger against himself than anyone around him. "You don't know my mother very well, do you, Reverend?"

"Maybe I don't. And, I need to change that. Other shiny things distracted me when I should have been getting to know my parishioners better. Especially upstanding members of the community, like your mother. In fact, I came here to ask her about reinstating the Sunday School, and asking the children to help whilst we recruit new churchwardens."

"Mother would be delighted to hear about Sunday School. I'm not sure you'll get many takers though."

"But I've heard you are recruiting well into Beavers. There are more children on the island these days, what with all the new estates —"

Jake interrupted me. "But that's very different to forcing the Bible down their little throats."

Orla, now fully dressed, stepped forward. "And that's why we can't recruit to the Brownies. I mean, we have lots of little girls sign up for Rainbows. Well, it's their mothers mainly. But as soon as they go to school and hear about what the Beavers and Cubs do every Friday night, you know, fun stuff like learning to climb and light fires, we can't compete with embroidery."

The proverbial penny ran down the pinball machine of my mind. *Hadn't Ginny and Mary said they thought Orla had eyes for Simon Banks? Their subterfuge had worked well, but why did they think it was necessary?* "So that is why you think your Mother will disapprove of you both? Some rivalry over your being the leader of the Beavers!"

"If only it was just that." Jake's pink cheeks puffed. "I'm not my father, you see? I turned my back on the Boy's Brigade, and Sunday School and Orla's a Catholic!"

"But Orla runs the Rainbows?" I protested, sure that no member of my church could hold with such petty bigotry.

"That's one thing. Leading her wayward son even further astray is quite another. I tried to talk to her before, but what she didn't call Orla... it made me blush."

"I'm no strumpet." Orla tucked her blouse into her skirt waistband. "Despite what you just witnessed. Promise us, Reverend, that you won't tell her."

"I promise. But I feel a sermon about tolerance, love, and acceptance coming on."

Jake's eyes rolled upwards. "Oh, please no, I beg you."

"Where's your mother now?" I sighed.

Orla looked at her watch and pushed past me. "Setting up for Brownies. I need to get back or she'll notice I've gone."

Jake's admiration followed the Rainbow Leader as she ran back around to the front of the hall. "You have no idea who my mother is, Reverend Ward. No idea at all."

***

I walked into the hall to the sound of a familiar anthem. Excited children's voices punched a compelling melody above a back-beat of a dozen rubber-soled feet, each jostling for the best seat on the wooden hall floor. Mary Meadows conducted them from in front of the hatch to the kitchen.

A loud clap signalled their symphony of chaos to a close, and they all sat up straight like meerkats on sentry duty. Some prize, or other, was on offer for the best behaved.

"Girls!"

Mary's shrill voice even made me stand to attention.

"Look, we have a visitor. What do you say?"

Two short rows of yellow caps with matching ponytails beneath turned and, in one voice, proclaimed. "Welcome to First Wesberrey Brownies, Reverend Ward."

Smile, Jessamy. Nothing Children of the Corn about that.

"Thank you, girls. Don't you all look smart in your brown and yellow uniforms. I was a Brownie here as well, you know, but we wore mud brown dresses and a felt beret. Your uniforms are much nicer." I picked on an eager girl in the back row with a sash full of badges. "That's quite the haul you have there. Darcy, isn't it? I have seen you reading at the school assemblies. You were very good."

"Thank you, Sir, I mean Miss."

The rest of the girls giggled.

Mrs Meadows clapped her hands loudly, and order immediately returned.

"That's okay. Many people see my uniform and get confused about what to call me. But, though I may be in a job that was traditionally held by men, there are lots of female vicars now. Sir. Miss or Reverend, I'll answer just the same."

"As long as you're not one of those *they* and *them* people. Utter nonsense, we'll be addressing each other as *it* before long. Heaven forbid." Mary folded her arms across her chest, holding in her outrage as much as possible.

"Everyone has the right to refer to themselves as they wish, Brown Owl. We are all God's creatures, are we not? Love one another and all that jazz."

Mary grunted. "Was there something in particular you wanted, Reverend Ward?"

"Yes, Mrs Meadows there was." I steered my gaze to the children. "I'm looking for volunteers to help with the collections and the hymn books at mass over the next few weeks. I'll need lots of helpful hands and who are more helpful than Brownies, right?"

Eager arms shot up. Orla took note of those interested and agreed to talk to their parents later.

"Will you stay a while, Reverend, and help with the baking?" she asked. "We're doing something a little different for the bazaar this year. The girls are very excited."

"I would love to, Orla." I smiled at the cherubic Brownies and then back at Brown Owl. "So, what treats have you got in store for us?"

Mary unfolded her arms and struck a full-on Wonder Woman pose. Hands purposefully on hips and legs confidently astride. "Doughnuts. The Scouts will never think of making them."

Gloria In Excelsis Deo

My dreams that night featured doughnuts. *I can't think why...* dozens of Krispy Kreme boxes faced up on the battlefield against Dunkin' ring doughnuts fresh from the fryer. Children and adults alike ducked behind stalls in the church hall as churros rained down upon them. There was jam and sprinkles everywhere. Neither side had the advantage. It looked like a sorry tale of stale batter mix until Mrs Fisk rode in on a penny-farthing lobbing last year's rock cakes down on the dazed parishioners below. Victory secured, her husband carried her aloft to the giant Norwegian Blue in the church apse behind the altar, where she placed their gold star.

I needed a coffee to go with all those doughnuts.

I found Tilly slumped over a bowl of cereal, her face inches from the rim of the bowl.

"Wake up, sleepy head. You almost had a cornflake facial."

"Eurgh? Sorry, late night. I went over to your sister's after work to look at her merchandising ideas."

I pointed at the coffee machine. "Is that fresh?"

Tilly pushed some loose curls back from her forehead and yawned yes. I filled a mug and took my space at the other end of the kitchen table. "Hugo's gone out already. I'll walk

Alfie when I'm dressed. Do you have any exciting plans?" She mumbled into a spoonful of milk and golden flakes.

"Christmas assembly. In the church. We will be setting out the nativity scene. All except the baby Jesus, of course."

"Yeah. Right. Because he isn't born yet. That's so cute, really."

I agreed it was. "Tilly? I know we haven't spoken about it much, but do you have any concerns about how things will change when Lawrence moves in?"

She wiped some milk off her chin with the knuckle of her right hand and took a beat. "It's your home. I'm just a guest."

"But I hope you see it as your home too. I don't want you feeling awkward."

"You mean more awkward than moving in with the woman who exposed my father as a people trafficker? I think we have moved beyond awkward, don't you?" She took a deep breath. "Jess, I love being here. You've made me so welcome. Everyone's been amazing. I adore Luke. I admire you. Your mother and aunts are incredible. Rosie is inspiring and Zuzu is, well, Zuzu. You are like family to me. But I have a mother and I am going to university soon. How I feel about Lawrence moving in is irrelevant. All that is important is that you want him to. And you are marrying the guy, so I guess you do."

"Oh, I do. I can't wait."

"Well, there's nothing else to worry about. So, we won't talk about this again. Okay?"

"Of course, I promise." Talking of promises... "Tilly, do you know Orla Kerrigan?"

"Yeah, she comes into the Cat and Fiddle sometimes, why?"

"Did you know she's seeing Jake Meadows?"

Tilly sniggered. "Of course. Everyone knows. Well, except his mother. But don't worry, she won't find out. That's the great thing about Wesberrey. People know how to mind their own business."

"Which reminds me, you'll have the place to yourself tonight. I'm staying overnight on the mainland with my sisters."

"Yeah, Rosie mentioned it. Luke and I have the run of two houses after work." Tilly laughed. "We're spoilt for choice. I think we will probably come here if that's okay with you. Keep the furballs company, especially as Lawrence is staying overnight in the big smoke."

"Be my guest." Only semi-caffeinated, I pushed back my chair and beelined to the coffee machine. "Right, I need a second cup, and I think I crave something more substantial than a bowl of cereal. Do you fancy an egg?"

"Well, if you insist." Tilly strolled over and joined me at the stove. "Jess, can you make sure none of you goes missing tonight?"

"I have no intention of being a vanishing bride. Scrambled or boiled?"

***

I watched from the side as Lawrence led the school children in an orderly file up the nave and splintered classes into pews on either side, filling the first five rows. This time next year, we will fill ten rows with ease. With all the scheduled improvements to the school in full flow, many parents were eagerly adding their children's names to the waiting list and new classes were planned to accommodate them. In fact, that was why Lawrence had to go to London later that afternoon for a breakfast meeting at the architect's office the following day. With all the school activities in the run up to Christmas, that was the only time he could meet them. I was missing him already.

I recognised Darcy from the night before. She had both a yellow metal *Prefect* shield and a red one saying *Librarian* on her sweatshirt. *That girl liked badges!*

"Good Morning, Miss."

"Good morning, Darcy. Are you going to introduce me to your friends?"

The young girl named all her associates like she was listing off the merit awards from her sash. "This is Beatrice. She loves dogs. Stella's into K-pop and Kayley wants to be a Disney princess."

"Kayley? Which princess is your favourite?"

"Arial, Miss."

"She's the Little Mermaid, right? You have red hair just like her."

"I know, Miss, that's why she's my favourite."

Fair enough. "I don't recall seeing any of you at Brownies last night?"

Darcy raised her hand. I granted permission to speak. "They're all Cubs, Miss. They say Brownies is bor-ring!"

"Hmm, but you enjoy it, don't you, Darcy?"

"Yeah, it's alright. But I prefer Cubs, too.

"Ah, you go to both. Do you have as many badges from Cubs as well?"

"Probably. I haven't counted them. But I will and I'll let you know."

The girl she called Beatrice nudged her companions and whispered something in Kayley's ear. An infectious giggle spread between them.

"What's so funny?" I asked.

Kayley looked wildly at the others. "I don't think we should say it out loud. In church, you know. Jesus might be angry."

"Well, if Jesus is going to be angry, he already is, because he can hear your whispers." I pointed out, half in jest.

The girls huddled together. Darcy pulled away and smoothed down her skirt. A big confession was coming. "Beatrice said Cubs is better because Mr Banks is a hottie!" Her hand rushed to her mouth to stop any more revelations from spilling out.

"Well, girls, I don't think God will be angry at you for admiring one of his creations, do you?" I smiled. "Though, you know you shouldn't judge people for their looks, good or bad." The girls bobbed their heads in agreement. "And, girls, please stop whispering in church. From now on, Beatrice, don't be afraid to speak up. Jesus knows what's in your heart, so you might as well be proud of what you have to say.

"Yes, Miss," they answered in unison.

"So, are you all baking cakes this afternoon with Mr Banks?"

Beatrice opened her mouth as if to answer when a familiar voice sliced through our conversation. Audrey Matthews, formidable school secretary and my erstwhile arch nemesis, called for everyone's attention from the steps of the altar.

"That's my cue. Girls, it was good to chat. See you at the bazaar tomorrow and may the best team win. Eh?"

"Oh, that will be the Scouts, Miss. Mr Banks is the best."

Well, well, Mr Banks, you have quite the fan club.

I joined Lawrence, Audrey and the other teachers by the altar and motioned to Rosemary, who had been patiently waiting at the organ console in the upper nave, to begin the first hymn.

Air filled the pipes and over the tune of the first line, I announced. "Our first carol today will be 'O Little Town of Bethlehem'."

***

We ended the assembly with a stately procession of nativity characters to a lively rendition of 'Angels We Have Heard on High'. *Everyone loves to go all out on the Glorias.* Each child placed their ceramic figurine in the miniature stable with a reverence that spoke to the magic of Christmas. Many of these young people were following in the footsteps of their parents and their grandparents before them. Generation upon generation of families celebrating the birth of our Lord.

Not that my family had a history of Christmas celebrations. I took part in school activities and, like many of the children in front of me, that was the only time I stepped inside a church. When we moved from the island, and I started secondary school, I didn't think twice about the lack of church-based activities in my comprehensive, multicultural, secular education. We celebrated all faiths and their associated festivals.

When I worked in an inner city parish, there were strong community links with the local temples, mosques and synagogues. In fact, when some local yobs targeted the mosque with a series of petrol bombs, the then parish priest opened the doors and allowed them to worship inside the church. I can recall my job was to drape a cloth over the Christian images on the walls to provide a more suitable place for them to pray and we used some metal framed hospital dividers in storage from the regular mother and baby clinic to create a safe space for the women to sit separately. It didn't matter they were on a different path to God. He was the same deity, and we were one community. They were our neighbours, and it was the Christian thing to do.

Now, of course, I know all paths lead to the same place. Pagan, Hindu, and followers of The Force. The key is love, and that is what I plotted my talk around. Love. The gifts the three wise men bring to the new-born king came from a place of love. Love brings hope. With love in our hearts for our friends and family, we can overcome every challenge, no matter where we find ourselves. The Magi did not judge Jesus on his humble beginnings, for they recognised the love they felt for him and knew he was the one. Jesus loves us too, no matter who we are, because of that light of love that lives within each of us.

As my speech finished, I fanned out the fingertips of my right hand to my fiancé and found he was, at the same time, reaching out for mine. The frisson when they met, though brief, sent delicious ripples of joy along my arm and through my body. I was certain the rows of children before me could see the warm, fuzzy glow in my heart.

Maybe they didn't register any change, but out of the corner of my eye, I could see that Audrey had noticed. And a rare Christmas miracle — I caught her smiling!

The assembly over, I chased my nemesis to have a quick word before she headed back to the school.

"I can't hang around, Vicar. I need to get the registers checked."

"Of course, Audrey, I don't want to keep you. I was meaning to ask you earlier, but things have been so busy what with the run-up to Christmas and so on."

"And your wedding preparations. Only a fool would get married on Boxing Day. Not that I'm calling you a fool, but..."

"No, you're right. We're totally crazy. So, I'll understand if you say no, but, well, Saturday night, I'm going to have a few drinks in the Cat and Fiddle, sort of like a hen night, I suppose, and I would be honoured if you would join me."

Audrey's jaw plummeted to the top button of her blouse. "I, I, I... Are you, I mean, erm, I guess, yes. Yes, Reverend Ward. I would love to accept."

I clapped with more excitement than her acceptance warranted. "That's great, then. Around seven o'clock? Phil's letting me have the function room at the back."

As Audrey wandered off, I knew she would be running my invitation over and over in her mind all day. *I'm sure she thinks I'm totally mad! But it's the season of love, after all.*

Return To St Mildred's

F riday evening brought with it the promise of pre-wedding merriment with my sisters. We started with a meal in a quaint Italian restaurant and then headed back to the rented cottage with one important pit stop. We interrupted our journey to call in at the pub Tabitha, Ruben and LaKeisha said they took Muriel to the night she disappeared. Ideally, we would keep well away from the non-alcoholic spirits tonight, but my gut was telling me we were in for a bumpy ride.

The bar staff at the local hostelry in Oysterhaven remembered the night Muriel went missing and the parapsychology students hitting the bar just before closing with a 'strange lady in a velvet cloak', whom they agreed was behaving weirdly.

The balding landlord, whose pot-belly suggested he sampled a lot of his own wares, told us as much, whilst he pulled a half pint of pale ale for Rosie. He nodded to our left. "She was terrified of the slot machine. Kept muttering incantations or some such nonsense under her breath every time it lit up."

I glanced over at the flashing lights of the fruit machine and frowned. "Maybe she was just superstitious?"

The landlord shook his head. "I'd say she was more than that, miss."

"Really?"

He flicked a dishcloth over his right shoulder and gazed at the wooden beam above the bar as if it held a playback video recording of the encounter. "She had something about her. A glow. You don't forget a young woman like that."

"I guess not," I replied. "Er, you said *young* woman?"

An old soak who was propping up the bar in the opposite corner slid over to join us. "Yeah, she was a strange one. We get all sorts in here."

"Including you, eh, Alfred!" the landlord quipped.

"Not so much of your cheek, or I'll take me custom elsewhere." Alfred nodded at his empty glass. "Now, ladies, don't mind if I do. Pint of Spitfire, please."

Zuzu dived into her purse and pulled out a twenty pound note. "Bar-keep, get this fine man a pint and take one for yourself." Alfred smacked his lips as the landlord lined up a clean glass under the tap. Zuzu intercepted the pint as it landed on the drip mat. "So, Alfred. May I call you, Al?" My eldest sister edged in beside the old man, who was powerless to resist her. "Tell me exactly how strange this young woman was."

Alfred tugged at his collar. "She had an aura. If you like. I mean, she glistened. But that could have been perspiration under that heavy cloak. She wasn't like her companions. They were typical youngsters. Cheeky, bordering on rude. But she was... demure. That's the word. Demure."

Rosie pulled out her phone and searched for 'demure'. "Shy. Bashful. Humble. Meek. Meek like a sixteenth-century nun?"

"Yeah. Like a nun. She was talking in Latin. I recognised it from school. Went to the local grammar. I haven't always spent my time propping up the counter."

The landlord chuckled over a bowl of peanuts he was refilling. "Tell 'em, you were going to be a doctor, but they didn't like the look of your face."

"Well, they didn't." Alfred protested as he wiped the foam from the rim of his glass. "They said it was too gnarly. Patients wouldn't warm to me."

Zuzu stroked the old man's face with her manicured fingers. "How rude! I don't think your face is gnarly."

"Thank you, Miss. But the younger me lost all confidence. I let my grades slip, took to the drink and well..." He waved his pint glass in the general direction of the saloon bar. "The rest is, as they say, history."

"But I suspect," Rosie picked up the conversation. "Your time here has made you very good at reading people. I run a little café on the Island and you can tell so much about a person from what they drink. What did you make of this group?" To be inclusive, my sister's curious eyes darted from Alfred to the landlord and back again.

The landlord sniffed a reply. "She, the nun-lady, only wanted some water. The others ordered pretentious ales, as you would expect from people from the university."

"And there wasn't an older woman with them?" I asked.

"Nope, just the four of them."

The abrupt manner of the response told us the subject was closed. We thanked Alfred and the landlord for their kindness and took our drinks to the snug.

Rosie stabbed the ice in her drink with a plastic stirrer. "So this nun must be the actress you mentioned. It obviously wasn't Muriel."

"But there is no actress." Zuzu reached into her pocket and pulled out the key to the cottage. "Dave isn't ecstatic about us staying there tonight, but he knows better than to try and stop me. He's convinced there was no foul play and no actress."

"Did he challenge the other two groups about her?" I popped a couple of peanuts I had snuffled from the jar on the bar into my mouth. "I mean, the Psychic Society and the Spirit Sleuthers. Did he question them about her specifically?"

Zuzu sighed. "He didn't think it was pertinent to the case. Surely they would have mentioned if another person was there when he interrogated them, especially after Muriel had gone missing. The Psychic Society has used her services for years." I went to interject, but Zuzu raised her hand to stop me. "However, he did ask his junior officers to call around all the local talent agencies to see if anyone was booked out for the night and nothing, not so much as a stripper-gram. No actresses were roaming around Oysterhaven that evening in search of a role."

"That we know of." Rosie flipped the end of the stirrer into her mouth and then removed it, leaving it hanging between her fingers like a Twenties cigarette holder. "If the nun wasn't an actress, then who was she? The woman who came with the university group to this pub was young and *demure*."

"And" I added, "actress or not, she clearly wasn't Muriel. So, what happened to our mystic friend? She couldn't have vanished into thin air."

Zuzu had intel to share, but was torn between telling us what she knew and ordering another drink. "Same again?" We nodded. "Right, well, ponder this, my sexy siblings, whilst I get in the next round. Dave told me that the Spirit Sleuths were the last to leave the cottage, and they are certain that no one else was there. They did a thorough sweep through every nook and cranny as part of their investigation both before and after the event. They're adamant there was nowhere Muriel could have hidden away. No trap doors, no hidden cupboards, no priest holes. The place is tiny, with solid stone floors and walls. And nothing could move upstairs without the floorboards creaking. The place is six hundred years old."

"I guess we can check that out ourselves later." I crunched the last lump of ice from my drink between my teeth. This mystery made no sense. I trusted that Dave had asked all the necessary questions, but he... or rather, we were missing something.

When Zuzu returned, the conversation morphed naturally into one about wedding night jitters and talk of dresses, make-up, and hair. This time next week was Christmas Day and the day after, I would become Reverend Jessamy Pixley.

We walked arm in arm back to the cottage. The brisk night air drove away the lulling effects of a late evening spent sipping alcoholic beverages by a log fire. For a moment, we were like children again. Three sisters skipping back home after a night out. Like a freshly beaten rug on a summer's washing line, each of us felt renewed. The age gaps between us meant that, over the years, these breezy times had been few, however, our shared memories and deep affection created an unbreakable bond. Family is forever. Love reigns eternal. Sisters always have each other's backs; especially as drunk heels struggle for purchase along cobbled pavements.

***

The second we entered the cottage, an unwelcome feeling fell over me. It was as if someone was watching us. Zuzu and Rosie could sense it too. We grabbed each other's hands. A terribly familiar nauseous lump set in the pit of my stomach — something was about to start. *If only my superpowers could predict what's about to go down. But then I probably wouldn't be here in the first place!*

Connecting with a Tudor nun who had a penchant for abducting young women was a less than ideal way to spend an evening. We had no way of knowing what would happen here. Yet here we were. I had to be firm, brave even, for my siblings. This was new to them. I am a psychic, of sorts. I have an ability, a gift, and experience with the paranormal. And my faith. I needed to remember that.

I looked around the cottage as we walked cautiously through to the kitchen. The caretaker had worked hard to welcome us. A fire blazed in the hearth. The large wooden table sat square in the centre of the room, was already laid out with a teapot and some cups. However, despite their efforts to create an Instagram-able setting for a romantic getaway, after dark, the kitchen presented as a dank, drab room.

Two wooden chairs sat with their backs against the wall, four others flanked the sides of the table. We each pulled a chair out and sat down. Fingers reached across the wooden surface till we held each other's hands. A circle of sisterly love. Minus the ghostly presence, it might have been quite nice.

We sat and waited for some spectral guests to arrive. I closed my eyes and welcomed the security of being there with my sisters, even if I felt responsible for their safety. I relaxed my mind. In the cold kitchen, heat poured from their bodies, wrapping me like a blanket.

Tilly's last words to me echoed around my head. *Everything's going to be alright! No one is disappearing tonight.* Then, the ground trembled, and a howling wind poured into my ears, pinging inside the bones of my skull.

It had begun.

A chill prickled down my spine. My chest tightened as if someone, or something, was boring a giant screw into my heart. I fought to reopen my eyes, but they stubbornly resisted. A deep rumbling surrounded us, and the floor shook harder.

I tried to speak, to warn my sisters. Nothing came out. It was as if the wind that swirled around us had stolen my voice. I could feel Zuzu's hand tighten around mine as she squirmed in fear. The sound of Rosie's whimpering breaths matched the rapid beat of my heart. Terror paralyzed us, sitting ducks in a storm of unknown proportions.

Then, as suddenly as it had started, it stopped. The silence was more terrifying than the wind. I cracked open my eyes to find my sisters looking back at me with matching expressions of confusion and relief. *What had just happened?*

The peace did not last long. Once again, I felt the weight of the ground cracking and rolling beneath me, angry that something had disturbed its rest. I could feel the fear in my sisters' bodies, and the same cramp in my own. I realised I had to get them out of there as quickly as possible. We were not in control.

But my middle-aged reflexes were not quick enough. Moments later, I was being dragged out of my body and into another realm. A plane in which my ethereal self floated above the cottage like a child peering into a doll's house. I could see my sisters still inside the kitchen. Still holding hands. Still strong against the whirling chaos around us. Anchoring me, or my body at least, to the earth below.

My eyes darted to a group of large black hounds winding their way through the fields that surrounded the cottage. They circled closer and closer to the cottage, barking menacingly.

Their howls echoed on the wind.

I could see the terror on my sisters' faces. I tried to push myself back down. It was as if I was dangling in a demonic spider's web. The harder I fought, the tighter the invisible ropes that held me aloft. I tried to scream out again, but it was pointless. Everything moved in slow-motion. I could only watch helplessly as the beasts closed in on the cottage. Their barks tore at my every nerve.

There was a bright flash of light, and then everything went dark.

The next thing I knew, I was being dragged away from the cottage by my hair. I kicked and screamed, but it did no good. The hounds were too strong. Dirt kicked up into my face and blood drizzled down my forehead. The hair on my head was being yanked out by the roots. My arms pulled away from my body and my heart ripped out of my chest.

It felt like my body was being torn in two.

I realised the dogs were mere shadows in the night. Though their growls were gruff and demanding, they were phantasms. I could feel them, hear them, but they were not physically there. There was nothing but air to fight against.

The trees below me stretched out their naked branches towards the night sky, silhouetted against the moon and the stars, trying to pull me back. I reached down with my fingertips. They moved further and further away.

Then the dogs pulled me through a mist. An overwhelming fragrance filled the air - sweet, feminine, cloying. Salty droplets clipped my tongue. My sister's tears, their fear, their terror? *Bizarre image - why do I think that?* Finally, above all the tastes and sounds, the stench of sulphur caught at the back of my throat.

Sister Elizabeth

"Welcome. We were expecting thee." A young woman dressed in a nutbrown habit, tied at the waist with a cream rope, gestured with her hands to the panting black creatures at her feet. "Be not afear'd. Mine dogs shalt not harmeth thee."

I checked my face and hands for signs of injury. There was no blood. Not even any perspiration. "Who are you?"

"Sist'r Elizabeth." She replied with a sly grin, as though the answer was too obvious to speak. "The mistress thou seeketh is not amongst us."

"Then why did your hounds drag me here?"

She pulled back her cowl and tutted. "They didst not draggeth thee."

"My bruises beg to differ." I snarled back.

"What bruises?"

I pushed back the sleeves of my woollen jumper. There had to be marks from where they had pulled at my arms. Nothing. "But... I felt it. Them. The dirt. Their teeth."

"The dogs hath led. Ye hath followed." The nun raised one hand and pointed behind me. With the other, she lifted her skirt a few inches off the ground and strode across to me. "Behold!"

I turned. Through a peach-coloured fog, I could see myself with my sisters still sitting around the kitchen table, holding hands. Our eyes fast shut.

"Bid me, how can they bruise a body yond hast not moved?"

"I don't understand."

"Pray, pardon me. Ye hath heard tales of hellhounds and maidens, and thy fancy played out this scene as ye transition'd." *Really, all that was just my imagination?*

Sister Elizabeth pivoted to face me. Her eyes, two dazzling peridot discs, glinted in the half-light. "So, verily, I beseech thee, ask thy questions. The portal shall close soon."

The portal?

I expected my heart to still be racing, for my knees to be quaking. I was standing in front of a ghost. *Wasn't I?* Instead, I felt serene. Fire danced in her jewel-like eyes, but everything else radiated peace. "I'm looking for a friend of mine. Her name is Muriel."

"Aye, the lady wast here."

I waited for more. Nothing but an enigmatic silence followed.

"So, where is she now?"

"Back in thy realm."

Are all ethereal beings deliberately vague? "Yes, but where? She is missing, and her family and friends want to find her."

"The lady hast nay family. Living, at least. And her cater-cousins shall lief forget her." Sister Elizabeth clapped her hands. The dogs circled us. "T'is time for thee to return."

"No, please. Tell me where I can find Muriel."

The moon broke through the clouds, and a shaft of white light cast its glow upon us. The nun's skin glistened in the moonlight. *She has an aura! The woman in the pub —*

"T'wast me," she answered.

Of course, she can read my mind!

"Sister Elizabeth, I don't understand. When will I see Muriel again?"

The nun reached her hands up, grabbed the folds of material that sat on her shoulders, and pulled her hood back over her head. "The lady shall maketh herself known to thee."

The louring sky reclaimed the moon. Inky darkness enveloped us. When the clouds parted, I was alone. The pinkish-yellow haze that had separated me from my sisters wrapped itself around me and charmed my spirit back into its corporeal home. The return journey was pleasant, peaceful, powered by love.

"Jessie? Jess? I think she's coming back!"

I blinked my eyes open. "Was I gone for long?"

Rosie glanced over at the clock on the kitchen wall. "About five minutes. Felt like forever. You were in a trance."

"Rosie wanted to snap you out of it. But I knew you would come back when you were ready." Zuzu beamed. "I'm so proud of you."

"Proud of me?"

Rosie tapped her fingers on the back of my hand. "We saw it all. The dogs, the nun. Everything."

"So, you know, she didn't take Muriel."

They both nodded.

The screech of Zuzu's wooden chair on the stone floor rang loud enough to wake up the slumbering residents of the neighbouring cemetery. "I say we need another drink. Cocoa anyone?"

***

Less than half an hour later, changed into our pyjamas, we lay sprawled across the linen-covered sofas of the living room, mugs of hot beverages cupped in our hands.

After a quick game of I-Spy, to lighten the mood, Rosie steered the conversation back to our investigation. "What I still can't work out is how Muriel swapped places with Sister Elizabeth in front of so many sceptics? The parapsychology unit, those ghost hunters, whatever their name... "

"The Spirit Sleuths." I offered,

"Yeah, whatever. Even the Psychic Society. I mean, surely, they would be super observant of any paranormal shenanigans."

"Maybe they saw something but didn't realise they had." Zuzu swung her legs down from the arm of the chair. "I mean, we know now that Muriel crossed over just as you did, Jessie. We were holding hands, and we saw everything. Maybe they experienced the same thing but didn't realise what was going on. Or, because they don't possess our abilities, couldn't interpret it in the same way. It doesn't matter. Muriel came back. As you did. The only difference was that time Sister Elizabeth went on a bit of a pub crawl first."

"Yes, but how? Jessie's body stayed here." Rosie's legs closed like a fan as she, too, adopted a more thoughtful pose. "We saw the whole thing. Jessie, you didn't morph into a ghostly novice. People saw Sister Elizabeth. They physically interacted with her."

"And that still doesn't answer where Muriel is now." I followed suit, dropping my feet to the floor.

We sat, mugs in hand, facing each other, waiting for inspiration.

Rosie broke the silence. "Right, so only the university students and the people in the pub saw the nun. The others only saw Muriel. If the swap happened the other night just as we witnessed, then it looks like Sister Elizabeth took Muriel's place and they swapped back when the group returned to the cottage. Muriel was so traumatised by the experience she ran away."

"That would make everything fit. The Charmed sisters remain convinced Muriel is still alive. I haven't been able to contact her deceased spirit and Sister Elizabeth says she's back here, somewhere. Dave is correct. There is no crime and no foul play." I swirled around the dregs in the bottom of my mug. "I guess that's another mystery solved."

"Hardly solved. I mean, don't get me wrong, I am deliriously happy to know the old bat is alive, but how do we know she's safe and well?" My eldest sister slid off the sofa and parked her shapely rear on the floor, spreading her legs into a V-shape. Placing her empty mug to the side, she then raised one arm up and over to the opposite leg. "Sorry, need to stretch."

"Don't mind us." I giggled.

"You can join me if you wish." Zuzu twisted her torso across to reach the other side.

"No, we're good." Rosie and I replied in unison.

"I guess we just have to have faith." A lion-sized yawn followed. "I could say a little prayer for Muriel. If you want to join me?"

Zuzu and Rosie were of one mind. "No, you're good."

The Morning After the Night Before.

The caretaker had filled the cottage's fridge with breakfast items. To go with the now admittedly rather stale croissants, we had local butter (as well as a vegan alternative), preserves, milk from a nearby farm and some eggs. As Rosie had converted to full veganism, Zuzu and I took the milk and eggs to make an omelette.

"We have meat-free sausages. Do you want to cook them?" Zuzu passed an unopened packet to our sister, who sliced through the wrapping with a knife.

"Thanks. You know, I don't miss meat at all. Who would have thought it, eh? I mean, look how our lives have changed in the past year. All because, Jessie, you decided to come back to Wesberrey."

I cracked an egg into a clean mug. "Yep, and to think I really didn't want to. And Mum... she was totally against the idea."

"Well, at least we all know why now." Zuzu waved a spatula around as she spoke. "I invited her to the flat for lunch last week. Wanted to say sorry for being a brat when I was younger. I wasn't always the easiest child."

I snaked my left arm around her waist and squeezed. "Don't beat yourself up, Sis. You were the eldest. You saw stuff going on. You heard the rumours. Rosie and I were still kids. We didn't have a clue how Dad was behaving."

Zuzu shook me off. "I should've protected Rosie. I ran away with the first boy that asked me and I have been running from guy to guy ever since." She caught a sniff on the back of her hand.

Rosie had found another frying pan for the sausages and was standing behind us, sausages in one hand and pan raised in the other. "Am I going to need to use this to knock some sense into you?" she joked.

Zuzu turned to face her, half hysterically laughing, half hysterically crying. "I love you, you know that, right?"

Rosie lowered the pan. "Yes, I know. But I'm starving, so either get back to cooking or let the professional see the stove."

With that special sibling telepathy that owed everything to being family and nothing to our special powers, I took that as my cue to pull Zuzu away from the oven and guide her to the sofa.

"I'm sorry. I just need a moment." My eldest sister patted my leg as we sat. It was unusual to see Susannah like this. She was more inclined to pull out the compact from her bag, retouch her war paint and soldier on. Even with family, we rarely saw her being vulnerable.

"Sis, take all the time you need. We've got you." I glanced over my shoulder to check in with my baby sister. "Rosie's a better cook anyway. I burn water."

Zuzu shuddered. "The girls are going to be here in a few hours. I need to, er, you know."

I pulled my older sister close. Her blonde head flopped on my chest. "I can't wait to see Phoebe and Chloe again. It's been too long. It's their first time on the island, right?"

My blouse caught Zuzu's soggy reply. "I'm scared, Jessie. I haven't really seen either of them for years. They aren't like Freya." She pulled back and rigorously rubbed her tears away. "She's like you, you know. Gentle. Forgiving. I wasn't there for them, you know. I left them with you and Mum, for heaven's sake. Jessie, you were more their mother than I was."

"You did what you had to do. No one blames you."

"Mum did. They did. I do."

"But we are all going to be back together this evening. For Christmas. For my wedding."

"Yeah, and for your hen night. They are here for you, Lil Sis. Not for me." Zuzu bounced the back of her hand off the end of her nose, catching a few stray tears. "Anyway, no point feeling sorry for myself, eh?"

"Zuzu, you're allowed to feel. To be vulnerable. To let people in."

My sister smiled. "That's what Dave says too."

"Well, he's a very intelligent man. And the son of a Baron."

"And don't forget devastatingly handsome." Rosie called over from the kitchen table.

Zuzu rose with a little shimmy. "Oh, yes. And a beast in the bedroom!" She flipped her hair and snatched a centring breath. "Are you done fixing those sausages yet?"

Zuzu was back in the room.

My beautiful, tragic sister, who had sought love in all the wrong places, finally had her man.

We ate our breakfast and filled our conversation with talk about love and the men in our lives. Three men none of us had even met this time last year. How we had found them and ourselves by returning to Wesberrey. We may have also found out we have goddess powers, but above all, we have found each other again.

Now we had to find Muriel.

**

Cottage locked up, and the key returned to the caretaker, we grabbed a taxi to catch the next ferry. We all had a busy day ahead. Rosie disappeared into the cabin to snuggle up to Bob the moment the ferry cast off. When we docked, Susannah dashed to her marina apartment to prepare for her daughters' arrival a few hours later and I jumped in one of the horse-drawn carts heading towards the hospital.

A tinsel-covered Martha greeted me at the reception desk. "Season Greetings, Reverend. Santa is already making his rounds. You should catch him in the refectory, just past the x-ray department."

"Martha, thank you. Dr Sam with him?" And by 'him' I meant Phil. Our local pub landlord and jack of all trades had been dressing up as Father Christmas for years. First the hospital and later he would have a grotto at the bazaar in the church hall.

"Of course. She's dressed as an elf."

The prospect of seeing my willowy best friend dressed in a red tabard with her stringy legs in green tights was irresistible. I raced down the corridor.

"Ho, ho, ho. Merry Christmas!" Phil waved at me from across the hall. "Look who's just walked in. Reverend Ward, what do you want for Christmas?"

"Well, Santa, I just want everyone to be healthy and happy." I paused at the door and surveyed the room. An artificial tree listed in the corner, weighed down with the burden of flickering lights and dusty old ornaments. Phil, or rather Santa, sat on a makeshift throne to the side and lined up in front of him were patients and their visiting family and friends. Some of them were still in their hospital beds, wheeled into the hall for some Christmas cheer.

Sam stood by a stack of gaudily wrapped boxes, dressed, as Martha described, in full elf attire. Though her look was more *Lord of the Rings* than the *Miracle on 34th Street.* She looked majestic.

ENSHRINED EVIL

After a raucous sing-a-long to a pre-mixed tape of chart-topping Christmas songs and popular carols, it was time to hand out the presents. Phil played his part with relish. With his naturally white hair and twinkling blue eyes, it was as if he was born to be Santa. He paused and spoke with every patient. Asking them about their illnesses. Talking to them about their plans for when they went home — their hobbies and dreams. Making them laugh. Sam and I followed behind like faithful puppies, taking photographs when requested and passing out the presents.

I whispered to Sam how much I admired her outfit.

"Well, I knew you would be wearing a costume." She laughed.

"Eh? I'm wearing my normal uniform."

"Exactly."

I hit her playfully. "Well, you look beautiful. I didn't know you had this in your wardrobe."

"It's new. Leo and I went to a WOW convention."

"WOW?"

"World of Warcraft. I'm a healer."

"Of course." I smiled. Images of my best friend and her undertaker boyfriend spending the dark nights completing quests in an online fantasy world filled my heart with joy. "So, things are still going well. You know, there's still time to make it a double wedding."

Sam jagged her bony fingers into my shoulder. "That's never going to happen."

"Third time's the charm." I quipped. My friend's face flashed pink. "Dr Samantha Peasbody, sounds good."

"What makes you think I would take his surname?"

"You took the first two. You can't get all precious about it now."

91

Sam laughed. "True. We'll see."

"I'll take that. Do you have a few minutes later to chat before the bazaar?"

"Yeah, we can do lunch. I need to talk to you about Karen, anyway."

***

Lunch came from a tin of tomato soup warmed up in the microwave on the filing cabinet in her office. Sam served it in a mug with a garnish of salt and pepper croutons.

"Don't judge." Sam took her seat opposite me. "I wasn't expecting company."

I blew away the steam from my cup. "Hey, I love tomato soup." I took a tangy sip of the creamy red goop. "Great to hear things are working out with Leo. Going steady looks good on you."

"Fine, I get the point. You're about to tie the knot, so everyone must join you in matrimonial hell." Sam fished out a crouton with a teaspoon. "Both Leo and I have ridden that particular pony before and we are very happy the way things are."

"I understand. You said you wanted to talk to me about Karen. How is she?"

"Well, you would know if you'd talk to her."

"I've been busy, what with the run-up to Christmas and the wedding."

"And ghost hunting. I bumped into Rosie yesterday. She said you were all going to stay at the cottage in Oysterhaven."

"Yes, it was—"

Sam cut me off. "You can regale us all with your tales of derring-do at the pub tonight."

"Sam," I leaned forward and put my mug on her desk. "Is there something wrong? You appear a little..."

"Acerbic?" She chugged back the contents of her mug.

"Er, yes, I guess so. Have I done something wrong?"

She sighed. "You haven't done anything at all."

My best friend was right. I have barely spoken to Karen since she moved back to Wesberrey. I thought about her often and asked around how she was. Karen was renting out Barbara's old home, and I knew Sam was checking up on her. I had been busy, but I knew I used that as an excuse. I didn't want to see Karen because she would ask me to channel her daughter again.

"I can't talk to Ellen for her."

Sam pushed back on her chair. "Have you even tried?"

"She's moved on. Her spirit is at rest. I can't do it, Sam. I'm sorry."

"Karen's really struggling, Jess. I have suggested counselling, but she's not interested."

"Can you prescribe her something? You know, to ease the pain?" I fidgeted in my seat. I should have been more supportive. Sam and I were all Karen had left.

"That's not the answer and you know it. It will be even worse when you're married. All loved up with your man. You'll be even less available."

"I don't think getting married will change things that much." I protested.

"That's because you've never been married. Trust me. Everything will change." Sam pulled at her elfin sleeve and checked her watch. "I have my rounds to do and you have a bazaar to open."

"Karen will be at the pub tonight, though, right?"

Sam sprung from her chair and threw the dregs of her soup into the sink in the corner. "As well as about twenty other women. You've invited half the town."

I slipped next to my friend and helped wash up. "I promise I will make time for her, okay? But no channelling. We don't want any more guests popping by tonight, if you know what I mean."

Let the Battle Commence

Down in the church hall, Phil threw himself back into his seasonal role with gusto. Barbara, dressed as Mrs Claus, assisted. Her painted freckles and red polka dot mop cap suited her rosy-cheeked complexion. Wesberrey's festive power couple had an efficient system for wrangling the straggly tail of eager children queuing below the stage. Phil sat on a red velvet chair in the centre of the raised wooden platform and, when it was their turn, he would beckon to the next child in line to come up the steps and sit on his knee.

"First year I'm playing Mrs Claus for real," my bleach-blonde secretary giggled. "I hear the hospital visit went well. Sorry I wasn't there. I had to cover the lunches in the pub. Tilly didn't show up for her shift."

"She didn't? That's strange. I knew Luke was staying over last night. Maybe they overslept. You know what it's like when there are no grown-ups around to spoil the fun."

"Yes, oh, to be young again." Barbara smiled. "Still, it's unlike her not to let us know."

"No harm done. The three of us handed out all the presents without incident. Phil is an exceptional Father Christmas."

Barbara preened as she looked up at her man. "He was born to play this role."

The church hall was buzzing. I couldn't recall when I had seen it this busy before. Several parishioners had worked all year to craft items for their stalls. Amidst the decoupage and paper crafts, we had a couple of ladies selling crocheted gifts. I particularly liked the multi-coloured octopuses. *Or is that octopi?*

There were the obligatory preserve stands, though no 'Hudson's Homemade' this year. After Keith's reckless endangerment conviction, Judith had packed the business up and left the island to live with her cousin, Maureen. Rumour has it, they will both be waiting for him when he is released in eighteen months' time.

Aside from the tombola and the headache-inducing whack-a-mole, the other two stalls of note belonged to the Scouts and the Guides. The battle of the doughnuts was in full swing. Both tables appeared to do a roaring trade. I couldn't tell from the stage who would win the coveted prize of topping off the tree, but I could hear Ginny's call to action across the crowd. It was time to circulate.

"Roll up, roll up, sprinkle your own doughnut for a fiver!" The ebullient Guide leader called out to draw more attention to their wares. She had full command of the people below from her elevated sentry position on a requisitioned wooden chair "Vicar! Splendid turnout, don't you think? Best showing for years."

"I'll take your word for that, Miss Whitaker. Are you still certain of your win?"

"Absolutely. No doubt that the best team will out. Zero sign of the pox this time. We're at full strength. Our D-I-Y doughnuts are going down a storm."

D-I-Y? Oh, Do-it-yourself! Jess, you fool! At least I didn't say that out loud. "Can I try one?"

"Be my guest." Ginny grabbed the back of the chair and crouched slightly to angle herself for the dismount. She snapped her fingers. "Mary, give me a hand, dear. Not quite as nimble as I once was."

Mary obliged. "You shouldn't have gone up there to begin with, silly billy."

"Well, my siren call brought in the Vicar. Biggest catch of the day, eh?"

I laughed, waving my finger above the doughnuts on the tray before me. "Well, I can't play favourites, you know. I will have to go over and taste the Fisk's cakes as well." I swooped in on my prey, only to have it knocked out of my hand.

Mary Meadows glowered at me over the cake stand. "Reverend, you have to pick a side. This is war!"

"War? Mrs Meadows, please let me buy my doughnut. It looks delicious, and I'm sure it will be better than the opposition's." *Think Jess, what would Switzerland do?* "How can I honestly tell everyone to choose your stall, if I haven't sampled from both?"

"Darn good point there, Vicar!" Ginny picked up a serviette, used it to retrieve the dropped doughnut, and handed it to me. "Drive traffic our way. Based on your honest review, of course. That one's on the house. Not a bribe, you understand. All proper and above board."

"Thank you." I pointed to my dog collar. "Thou shalt not lie and all that jazz." I graciously accepted the paper parcel. "What toppings have you got?"

"Caramel sauce, white chocolate swirls or hundreds and thousands." Mary growled. *I think I've upset her. For a Christian woman, she has a strange moral code.*

"Caramel and white chocolate it is then. I find those tiny little coloured candy strands too hard on my teeth."

Mary drizzled the sauce over the doughnut, the paper napkin, and my hand. "Oops, Reverend. I'm terribly sorry."

"Mrs Meadows, seriously, there's no need to apologise. I can lick it off." I drew my sticky fingers to my lips. "Hmm, tasty."

"Don't patronise me, Reverend." Tears swelled above her lower lashes. "If you'll excuse me. Ginny, I'm so sorry." Mary picked up a separate serviette, dabbed both eyes and ran off towards the toilets.

Ginny pushed the chair she had been standing on under the table and turned to the guides that were assisting her. "Girls, I fear Brown Owl isn't feeling very well. I trust I can leave you in charge of the stall."

The Guides, pristine in their blue and navy uniforms, relished the opportunity to prove their mettle. They organised the younger girls for maximum doughnut sprinkling efficiency. I turned to walk away and spotted a yellow and brown baseball cap crawling out from under the tablecloth. The furtive brownie was pushing a cardboard box in front of her.

"Darcy?"

The box-shifter sprung up, almost dropping her haul in the process.

"Yes, Miss."

"You're helping the Girl Guides. I thought you'd want to be with your school friends and the hot Cub leader."

"They have a lot of helpers, Miss. My mum said Brown Owl's at the end of her tether and that doesn't sound good, does it? So, I thought I'd help her instead."

"That's very sweet of you." The box in her hand intrigued me. It looked different to the others stacked by the wall. "What's in the box? More doughnuts?"

Darcy scrunched up her forehead. Her eyes flitted from side to side as if she was weighing up the possible answers. "Er, yes. Miss. Do you want one?"

I waved the remains of the one in my hand. "No, I'm good for now, Darcy. Thank you. I hope Brown Owl feels better soon. Carry on the good work, girls."

It did not take long to find out where Darcy's box had come from. A stack of identical ones stood next to the Scouts' stall in the far corner. They were all empty. *That's why she was underneath the table!* Darcy had infiltrated the ranks of the opposition.

Whilst I stood pondering who was the instigator of this shocking covert operation, Fran Fisk pushed a paper plate bearing a ring doughnut into my chest. "Sorry, Reverend. Didn't mean to get sugar on your blouse."

I scooped up the plate in one hand and brushed off the offending sugar dust with the other. "No worries, Mrs Fisk. You are very busy over here."

"Yes, almost sold out, as you can see. Jake and Simon have gone back to the storeroom to get some more. Good thing we made extra. Though I could have sworn we had another box."

"Indeed." I bit into the golden ring. "These are delicious. And so fresh." *Sorry, Ginny and Mary, the Scouts' doughnuts are superior in every way.* "I guess you had the advantage, you know, making them last night."

"I guess so. I hear they're doing their best to mask the taste of theirs with sticky sauce and sprinkles. No need for that here."

Frank Fisk appeared from the store with two more boxes and dropped them on the table with a loud grunt. "Ouch, I think I've done my back in."

Mrs Fisk abandoned her station and rushed to her husband's aid. "Frank, dear, what on earth did you think you are doing? Where are the boys?"

"Simon and Jake? I haven't the foggiest." He puffed as he collapsed on a fold-out chair behind the table.

"But they said they were going to get more boxes from the store. You must have passed each other." She turned her frustrations on the scouts chatting by the wall. "Boys, I need you to take over. Use the tongs to put the doughnuts on the plates." Fran passed paper plates along the table. "No hands, boys, no hands! Where are all the cubs?"

"Mrs Fisk, I think you need to get Mr Fisk home or see Dr Sam at the hospital. You can never be too careful with backs. Let me go to find Simon. He can't have gone far. And I'll round up all the cubs and send them back here. Okay?"

"Thank you, Reverend. We'll stay here until you get back."

"My pleasure." I left to look for the missing cubs and their leaders. *They're probably up to no good if the Guides and Brownies are anything to go by.* First, I tried the storeroom, the toilet block and then the kitchen, casting an eye across to the stall as I passed in case I had missed them. From across the hall, Frank's grimacing face bore into my soul. He must be in considerable pain. *Poor man!*

Where is everyone? I weaved my way through a bunch of carol singers standing in front of the doorway. I realised I hadn't seen Orla either. Perhaps she and Jake were taking advantage of all the bustle and confusion of the bazaar to gain a little private time around the back. *They're not in the main hall, that's for certain.*

To keep the heat in, the main door was closed. I stepped towards the handle and bang!

My body jerked back.

I stumbled back onto one of the singers. Or I think I did. At the same moment, all the lights went out in the hall.

Frightened screams bounced off the walls as anxious parents and children panicked in the dark.

Phil's baritone voice called for calm from the stage.

"Ho, ho, ho. Quiet now. Please. Everyone. No need for alarm. Looks like we've had a power cut, that's all. Those naughty elves, always having a bit of fun. Can everyone with a mobile put on their torches?"

Hushed murmurs followed as my parishioners fumbled in their bags and pockets for their phones. I apologised to the owner of the feet I had just crushed and did the same.

Raising my phone to my face, I was just about to flip the screen when the lights returned.

A palpable sigh of relief filled the room. A relief soon pierced by a terrified shriek from the side of the hall.

The cast iron lock on the door leading into the church vestry juddered. Its heavy wooden panels bashed open, hitting the wall with force. A gush of cold air swept Orla Kerrigan into the hall.

She was screaming blue murder. *Literally.*

"It's Simon. I think he's dead!"

A Matter of Light or Death

From my place at the end of the hall, everything following Orla's announcement played out in slow motion.

The assembled crowd parted like the biblical Red Sea as Orla staggered towards the front of the stage, clearing a circle for her to collapse in.

Whilst anxious mothers squeezed their crying children to their breasts, Barbara wedged herself beneath the Rainbows' leader and fanned her with her polka dot cap. "Please, give the poor girl some air!"

Meanwhile, Father Christmas, a.k.a. Phil had leapt off the stage and ran into the church next door.

Every second counted. I pushed through the carol singers and weaved a path through the stalls to follow him, grabbing young Darcy as I passed. "Go to the hospital and tell them to send a doctor here straight away."

I paused at the oak door and called back into the room. "Everyone stay calm. Can someone please call the police? No one is to leave until they get here."

Behind me, I could hear dozens of voices calling the emergency services. *Perhaps I should have been more specific. We've probably jammed the switchboard!*

102

The bright fluorescent light of the church hall stood in stark contrast to the near darkness of the nave of St. Bridget's. I followed Phil through the north transept to the chancel and there we found Simon Banks lying under the Christmas tree.

Phil crouched down to take his pulse.

"Is he...?"

Phil shook his head. "Dead? Not on my watch." Phil checked for signs of injury. He pressed his ear to Simon's chest. "I can't find a pulse! Vicar, take this." Phil threw his red bobble hat in my general direction and wiped his mouth on the sleeve of his velvet jacket. "I'm going in."

I recall being taught once that the best way to do CPR is to sing along to the Bee Gee's 'Staying Alive'. You place the fleshy heel of your palm on the centre of the chest and lace the fingers of your other hand on top, then press down firmly in time to the Ha, Ha, Ha, Ha portion of the song's chorus and keep that rhythm going.

Phil must have learnt the same method because I could just make out the tune as he hummed to himself on each compression.

I felt useless. There was nothing else I could do until professional help arrived.

"Look at his hands." Phil puffed at the end of a verse.

Simon's palms had red patches of blistering skin.

"Looks like he's burned them on something. Maybe from the hot fat fryer they were using to make the doughnuts. He could have snuck in here to make a fresh batch. That would technically be cheating, but —"

Phil continued the compressions. "I think he was electrocuted." He nodded towards a green cable wire trailing around the base of the altar steps. "Probably the Christmas lights. I should have replaced them. They're older than I am."

Staying Alive slowed down. Phil was tiring.

"Here, let me take over." I pushed my churchwarden to the side and placed my hand an inch or two below Simon's woggle. "Ha, ha, ha, ha, Staying Alive, Staying Alive"

Phil seated himself on the closest bench, his forehead ploughed with deep furrows. "It's all my fault, Vicar. He's been out for too long. Where is the doc?"

"I'm sure Sam will be here soon. What I don't understand is why he was in here and what was he doing fiddling with the lights?" I thought about trying to connect with Simon's spirit. If he *was* dead, and ready to travel on, I might miss my opportunity. Was it rude to attempt to commune with someone in the afterlife whilst at the same time trying to pump blood through their heart? What's the correct etiquette in a situation like this? *Good Lord, I'm singing a disco anthem!*

Now was not the time to worry about good manners. *Jess, get a grip of yourself.* I took a deep breath. *Simon? Can you hear me?*

There was no reply. *That's a good sign, right?* I tried again, and again. Each time a little more frustrated that the last.

"Vicar! You're going to break his rib cage." Phil grabbed my hands away. "It's my turn again. You sit yourself down."

I stumbled back to the bench. Phil was right. This was taking too long.

It was a good few minutes more before Phil was relieved by Sam and her staff paramedics bursting through the door from the church hall.

"Stand away, Phil, we've got this." Within no time, the medical team had sticky pads attached to Simon's bare chest and were connecting electrodes to a defibrillator. "Stay clear, please."

Simon's body jolted.

Sam, still in her elfin dress, bent over to take his pulse. His eyes fluttered open — for a second. "He's alive."

My best friend pulled out a mini torch from her bag, pulled back his eyelids and shone the light into his pupils. "Thank goodness you were both here. You might have just saved his life."

I put my arm around Phil's back and patted him on the shoulder. "Santa here did most of the work."

"Well," Sam rose from the ground and glided towards us like the lady on the lake. "I can't think of a better Christmas present, can you?"

Phil shook off my hand and Sam's praise. "He wouldn't have needed my help if I had better maintained the electrics."

"We don't know what caused it. Let's leave this to the police." I guided my verger back into the light of the hall. Sam left Simon in her team's expert care and followed us to check on Orla.

We found the young Rainbows' leader hunched over a cup of sweet tea on the stage steps. Ginny and Mary had taken over nursing duties. Barbara was on the phone and waved across as we drew closer.

"Is he dead?" Barbara asked.

Phil shook his head.

"No, he's not dead." She spoke into her phone. "The paramedics are with him now." Barbara covered the mouthpiece on her mobile and mouthed 'Inspector Lovington'. "Reverend Ward has just come back. And Dr Hawthorne. Which one do you want to speak to?" She handed the phone to Sam, who walked away to talk.

"Barbara, I think you should get Phil a cup of tea. He's blaming himself, when in fact he's the hero of the hour."

My secretary's pride flushed out her cheeks, but concern filled her eyes. "Of course, Reverend. And something for you?"

"No, I'm fine. I'll go check on Orla. How is she?"

"Shocked. She hasn't said much."

"I need to know if she saw anything." There were so many questions whizzing around my head. What was Simon Banks doing in the church? Was there anyone else with him? Did Orla see or hear anything suspicious? Was this a terrible accident, or had someone tried to kill the popular Cub leader?

As if she could read my mind, Sam intercepted me. "Whoa, hold on a second. Leave Ms Kerrigan to me. Dave will be here in a few minutes. He said not to let anyone go or let anyone touch anything."

"I've already told everyone they couldn't leave, and only Phil and I went next door. Apart from doing CPR, we haven't touched a thing. This isn't my first rodeo." I snapped. The tension of the past half an hour was taking its toll.

"Okay, Jess." Sam stroked away a loose strand of hair that had caught on my lashes. "You need to take a breath and, I don't know, say a few words to the man upstairs, or whatever you do to calm down. Doctor's orders."

"I'm sorry I snapped. You see to Orla, I'll go check on the Fisks. Maybe you could also take a look at Frank's back. He put it out carrying boxes of doughnuts." I could feel the corners of my mouth curl at the craziness of the situation.

"Fine, I'll be there in a minute. Never a dull moment on Wesberrey, eh?"

I steadied myself. After all, this wasn't my drama. The Fisks must be really worried about their colleague. It was my job to offer them support.

It really is quite amazing how small communities rally around when tragedy strikes. The initial fear and panic had morphed into a communal stoutness of heart, quintessentially British. Barbara wasn't the only person busy in the kitchen. A small army of crafters made tea and sandwiches behind the kitchen hatch. Across the hall, Scouts and Guides handed out the last of the doughnuts — all thoughts of competition vanquished by the need to lift everyone's spirits. And unclaimed gifts from the tombola kept the smaller children entertained.

I found Frank Fisk where I had left him, unable to move from his seat. His wife sat beside him.

"Is It true? Is Simon... d-d-dead?" The elderly man, wracked with pain and anxiety, appeared to have aged ten years in the past thirty minutes.

"No, he was unconscious, but the medics are with him now. We think, perhaps, he was electrocuted."

Fran Fisk placed a comforting hand on her husband's knee. "How can that even happen?"

"I don't know, but Inspector Lovington is on his way, and I am sure he will figure it all out. Do you know what he was doing in the church?"

Fran twisted the end of her neck scarf. "Reverend Ward, I told you, I thought he and Jake had gone to the storeroom."

Jake? "Hasn't he come back yet?"

They didn't need to answer. The looks on their faces said everything. Both men left earlier together to fetch more stock and now Simon lay injured and Jake was missing.

"Mr Fisk, Dr Hawthorne will be over as soon as she can, okay?" *I'm going to see if I can find Jake.*

Hunt the Beaver

D ave Lovington strode up the path towards me. "Jess, where do you think you're going? I left strict instructions that nobody was to leave the hall till I arrived."

"Surely, you didn't mean little ole me," I replied, channelling a southern belle coyness Vivien Leigh would have been proud of.

His moustache twitched. "And why would you be exempt, may I ask?"

"Because... oh, never mind. I was about to look for someone who may be a witness."

"Really? And the name of this witness is?" Dave pulled out his black notebook from his blazer pocket.

"Jake Meadows. He's the Leader of the Beaver troop and was last seen heading to the storeroom with Simon Banks, the young man who was electrocuted."

"And Simon Banks is?"

"Leader of the Cubs."

Dave scribbled some notes. "Any rivalry between these two men?"

"Not that I know of. I mean. There is Orla Kerrigan. She and Jake are a couple, though it's a secret. From his mother, at least. She was the one who raised the alarm."

"And you think Mr Banks was jealous of their relationship?"

"I don't know. It's just something Ginny Whitaker said at the bridge night about Orla having eyes for Simon. That seems very strange now."

"Right. And who is Ginny Whitaker?" Dave paused and rested his back against the lamppost that stood on the grass to the side of the path. It was spluttering into life as the sun set over the horizon.

"She's head of the Girl Guides. She's inside with Orla. They're by the stage with Brown Owl, I mean Mary Meadows."

Dave flipped back a page of his notebook. "Meadows? Any relation to our fugitive Beaver?"

"Yes, she's his mother." I was enjoying being the font of all knowledge. I didn't know much, but I knew more than Dave and I found it deeply satisfying.

Dave ran a hand through his hair. The electric light above picked out its amber flecks. I remembered, not so long ago, that very image made my knees go weak. Back then, I struggled to concentrate. Now I think of him as my brother. I loved Lawrence. I also found that thought deeply satisfying. "So, let me get this right. She doesn't know about her son's relationship with Miss Kerrigan. And... you called her Brown Owl, so she's in charge of the Brownies, correct?"

"Spot on, you're a quick study."

"It's my job," he smiled. "Beavers, Cubs, Guides and Brownies. How does Miss Kerrigan fit into all this?"

"She runs the Rainbows group."

"Of course she does. But no Scouts."

"Well, The Fisks, Frank and Fran, are inside too. They all are. It was the Christmas Bazaar."

"Right. Stupid me. The reports we got were that there was a blackout and then Miss Kerrigan came in from the church saying Simon's dead."

"Yes. That's exactly what happened."

"And you were in the hall at the time and can vouch that all these characters were there too. The Fisks, Mrs Whitaker —"

"I'm not sure Ginny's married."

"*Ms* Whitaker. Mrs Meadows?" Dave's eye twitched. I shared his frustrations. He wanted to get all the information he could before entering the crime scene, and I wanted to get on the trail of Jake Meadows before nightfall.

"Actually, now you mention it, they weren't. The Fisks were. Most definitely. Frank had pulled his back, and they were staying by their stall. But Ginny and Mary had left a few minutes earlier. Mary was upset about something, and Ginny ran off after her. But they might have come back in before the lights went out. I'm not sure."

"So, at the time of the power cut, you can't confirm the whereabouts of four individuals. This makes them persons of interest, and I will speak to them first. Thank you, Jess, you have been most helpful."

"As usual?" I smirked.

"Hmm, we'll see. Now, I'll let you go back to the vicarage. Zuzu is there. With her daughters. You have a hen night to get ready for, I understand."

The hen night!

"I'll have to cancel. Phil's pretty shook up. I can't imagine partying, to be honest."

"That's a shame. They spent hours getting ready." Dave's word caught on the back of his throat. His eye twitches accelerated.

Meeting Zuzu's daughters must have been stressful for him. "How did it go?" I asked.

Dave flipped his notebook shut and spoke into his blazer as he put it away. "They are all very lovely."

"Let me guess. Freya, of course you know already. Phoebe and Clara, well... don't take it too personally if they seemed a little aloof. My sister's track record with men is, how can I put this..."

"Erratic, chaotic?"

"Er, yes, I guess. But also tragic, and I'd say optimistic. Zuzu has been searching a very long time for what she has found with you."

"You think this time is different?" Dave kicked at the earth with his toes. "I really hope it's different."

"I know it's different. In time, Phoebe and Clara will see it, too."

"Anyway, I'll let you go, as long as you walk straight to the vicarage. I will watch you from here. No Beaver hunting, Jess." He chuckled.

I wanted to swoop him up in my arms and tell him how much my sister loved him. How she was more nervous than he was about her daughters' reactions. That he was the best man she had ever known, and he had nothing to worry about, now or in the future. Instead, I mumbled. "I promise."

***

Dave's watchful gaze followed me all the way home. I waved back from the front door and walked inside.

Alfie's ball rolled down the hallway and landed at my feet. His golden body careened after it. The drool from his jaws told me he had found a wonderful new friend to play fetch with. I followed him as he ran back into the kitchen. Phoebe, my strikingly beautiful (should be a model — after all, she has the height) niece, plucked the ball from his mouth, lifted it to throw again, and paused.

"Aunt Jess!"

"Who else were you expecting?" I laughed.

The most welcome sight greeted me from the kitchen behind her. All the women in my family gathered together. Three generations of sisters. Three from three. The power of three. You could cut the magic with a knife.

Freya sat closest to the back door, snuggling up to an unusually friendly Hugo. *He'd missed her, bless him.* Mum and Rosie, as expected, were busy making everyone something to eat. Zuzu was catching up with her eldest daughter, Clara. And sitting closest to the hall were my aunts, Pam and Cindy.

"Looks like I need to bring through a few more chairs from the dining room."

Phoebe grabbed my arm. "Hugs first. Come here."

It was my pleasure to oblige. I loved these girls as my own. Clara and Freya jumped up to join their sister. I thought my heart would burst with joy all over the vicarage kitchen. All thoughts of the events at the bazaar, hunting down Jake Meadows, or even chasing after Mystic Muriel shoved from my mind.

Over the welcoming squeals, one voice called us to order. "Jessamy, are you going to get those chairs? I want to sit down!"

"Yes, Mum."

Oh, What a Night!

Hen night formally cancelled, I slipped out of my vicar's garb and resigned myself to a quiet-ish night at home. *Would it be awful to admit I was slightly relieved?* The women I loved most were there in the vicarage. Sam even popped in after they airlifted Simon Banks to Accident and Emergency on the mainland.

"Jess, I am going to take a bottle over to Karen's. Keep her company. Leo was expecting to entertain himself this evening, anyway."

"Tell her I'll be over before the wedding. I just can't... I mean, my nieces have only just arrived."

Sam understood, but she also knew that Karen would want a friend. As for the rest of my guests, they had their own families to be with. I had spoken with most of them on the phone and they all understood the situation, even Audrey. Notwithstanding Simon's accident crushing the party mood, it was too much to expect Phil and Barbara to play hosts after what had happened.

"I'll tell her you'll try, okay? Best to not build her hopes up. You have a lot to do. It's Christmas and you have a wedding, remember?" She looked down at her dress. "I'd better go home first and change. Grab my pjs. We can have a sleepover. It'll be fun. Enjoy your evening."

"Sam, before you go. Do you think Simon Banks is going to make it?"

She sighed. "Jess, there was nothing more you could do. If he doesn't pull through, Inspector Lovington will be looking for a murderer. He found evidence that someone had tampered with the socket. This wasn't an accident."

***

I returned to the kitchen and made a theatrical cough to get everyone's attention. "Hey guys, why don't we move into the lounge? It's more comfortable in there."

No one stirred.

"Did Sam just say it wasn't an accident?"

I looked at Rosie and nodded. "Someone messed with the plug, I think. Who would do that?"

"Well, whoever it is, their fate can wait till morning." Mum rose from her chair and grabbed two plates of cheese and crackers from the table. "This is supposed to be your night, so let's go into the next room and relax."

I hung back to fetch some more nibbles from the cupboards and watched as my family walked down the hall. Noticeably, Cindy was not as nimble on her feet as before. At the doorway, Pam turned to offer her a steadying arm. Her rapid deterioration rooted me to the spot. When we first met, just under a year ago, in that very hallway, she could have put young Freya to shame with her energy and vigour. In fact, both of us had marvelled at her litheness.

Mum came back to get some glasses. "Freya's introduced her sisters to your drinks cabinet. I see you've restocked it."

"Well, it is nearly Christmas."

"I'm not judging."

Well, that makes a change. "Mum, Cindy is looking so frail. She should see a doctor."

"What for? Jess, it's merely an adjustment. You're using your powers more and hers are decreasing. Her body is playing catch up, that's all."

"So, she's not dying?"

"Sweetheart, we're all dying." Mum took a dishcloth from the drawer and wiped the rims of a glass. "When did you last clean these?"

"Not judging?" I joked. "It's only dust."

Mum tutted. "Jess, there's no need to worry. Cindy's just feeling her age. Yes, the decline has begun, but she should have years left yet."

"What if I stop using my gifts?"

"It doesn't work like that. Come on, let's go join the others. My family's reunited, and I'm not letting thoughts of death, or missing psychics or crispy Cub leaders spoil my evening."

"Mum! Crispy? That's awful."

"So sue me. Come along and grab those bags of crisps on the way."

***

Despite my mother's ardent wishes, talk soon turned to our search for Muriel and what happened the night before at the cottage.

Phoebe topped up her mother's glass. "So, did you tell Dave what went down?"

Zuzu squirmed. "I told him it had been interesting, and that all we had learnt really was that Muriel was still alive."

"But we knew that, darling!" Cindy retorted. "What's more interesting is that all three of you saw this Sister Elizabeth, yet only Jess crossed the veil. In our experience, that's peculiar."

"Maybe it's because when we have travelled, we have always visited our own. We were safe." Pamela suggested. "I've never witnessed hellhounds before. Her realm must be *outside*."

"Outside what?" Phoebe asked. I could see that both she and Clara were struggling with the concept. Hardly surprising, it had taken me the best part of a year to accept the truth about the Goddess, her triple wells and the idea that not only did they need protecting, but that it was down to us, well me, to protect them.

Clara, in particular, had always been a serious child and was more so now she was an adult. All our talk of psychics and goddesses was causing a storm of confusion and intellectual dissonance in her dyed auburn head. I could tell she was struggling because she was unusually quiet. I knew my eldest niece so well. If she didn't know what to say, she said nothing. Phoebe was more inquisitive — the advantage of being the middle child, I suppose.

Pam's reply was as enigmatic as always. "Outside of the realm of the Goddess."

"You mean hell?" I suggested. "After all, surely that's the opposite of heaven, or wherever the Goddess resides. Young women are being abducted. Not exactly cherubs and divine light."

Cindy waved for a refill. "This is surprisingly good wine, darling. I've never seen any cherubs. That's your lot. Angels and demons and stuff. The missing girls, though. My instinct tells me there's a clue there somewhere." Cindy took a sip from her glass. "What if Sister Elizabeth took Muriel by mistake, found out she was too old and sent her back? Now she's wandering around between the realms all confused."

Mum almost spat out her chardonnay. "Cynthia Bailey, you have completely lost the plot. Do you really think Muriel is some kind of zombie? I blame all that stuff you smoked in the Sixties. Killed off a few too many brain cells, if you ask me."

Cindy sprung up in her chair. "Oh, now that's an idea. I don't suppose any of you young people have any weed?" *That's more like the aunt I had grown to know and love.*

If my nieces had, they weren't telling.

Time to change the subject. "Let's just have another drink. And then, I might have to kick you all out. I have work in the morning."

"Jessie, you're so boring. I trust Lawrence is prepared to never have a lie in on a Sunday ever again. What a good way to ruin a weekend." Zuzu stood up and marched across to the fireplace. "I say we call one of those cute horse-drawn cabs and head back to my place."

Everyone agreed that was a great idea until Clara pointed out it was already one in the morning.

"Freya, come and help me get the beds ready. I have blankets a-plenty." I tugged at one of the said blankets from underneath my youngest niece. "And if you're all up early enough, you can join me for mass." I chose to ignore their groans.

***

With everyone snuggled up for what remained of the night, I retired to my room. Faith, family and friends — the trifecta on which I based my life. Cocooned in my bedcovers, I turned to the first to pray for the other two.

I had accepted the Goddess because of the faith I had in my God. It was not my place to question the why and wherefores of Christian versus pagan, monotheism versus polytheism, or even atheism. It was my duty, though, to take what I knew in my heart to be true and share the message with others. And I knew that my Lord and Saviour listened to my prayers, so I offered one up for Simon Banks's full and speedy recovery. I asked God to protect Muriel — wherever she may be. I asked the Almighty to watch over my loved ones. And thanked him for all the blessings in my life. For my family, my friends, my new life and my future husband.

Frantic scratching at the door interrupted my thoughts. I unwrapped myself and, in the low light of the sleeping moon sneaking through the cracks in my curtains, made my way across the room to open the door. Black fur streaked past and make itself at home on the foot of my bed. Alfie followed close behind his feline friend. Both cuddled together, leaving me a sliver of mattress and the corner of a duvet.

Love — that wonderful pink, fluffy feeling that binds us all together filled my heart. "Okay then, boys. But I'm warning you, there won't be room once Lawrence moves in, so make the most of it."

Entwined in a loving mass of black and yellow fur, they didn't care at all.

Purple Candles

L awrence and the school choir opened the service with a rousing rendition of *O Come, All Ye Faithful*. Rosemary treated us all to a mercifully short rendition of Schubert's *Ave Maria* on the organ during communion. And, as we lit the fourth purple candle on the Advent crown during the sermon, I encouraged all present to consider how like a flame was our precious gift of life. A sudden blast of air and it could be gone.

The police had taped off the area around the Norwegian Spruce with yellow and black *Police - Do Not Cross* tape. *Not very festive!* A stark reminder to those of us gathered before the altar at St. Bridget's of the fragility of life, and that for many, the holiday season can be as cruel as it can be kind, as painful as it can be joyous.

Unable to ignore the yellow and black elephant in the chancel, I decided, instead, to make it a feature of my sermon. We should all embrace the joy in every moment. I meant my words to be uplifting. *I hope I hit the mark.*

Closing prayers included a heartfelt petition to the Big Boss for Simon's good health and a call to all to wish each other a Merry Christmas. Some of the girl Cub Scouts broke down at the mention of their beloved leader's name. However, despite the tears, the final procession exited to an exuberant congregation singing *Go Tell It on the Mountain* accompanied by the school orchestra (well, six melodicas, some tambourines and Lawrence on acoustic guitar, to be exact).

As I stood at the church door, smiling and shaking hands with my flock, it was hard not to look at each one with fresh eyes. I considered the potential motives of each parishioner who passed. One of them orchestrated Mr Bank's near-death experience. *If only my psychic abilities stretched as far as a red neon arrow in the sky pointing to the perpetrator.*

Mary Meadows was the last to leave. She was alone. Her son, Jake, was not with her.

"Mrs Meadows, terrible business with Mr Banks. How's Jake this morning? Yesterday's events must have been quite upsetting." I used a two-hand handshake and secretly hoped my goddess powers would pick up on something, anything, as I clasped Brown Owl's palms in mine.

"Oh, yes, right, I suppose. He…" Mary paused. "Jake's a little under the weather today."

"I'm sorry to hear that. I'll be heading to Oysterhaven General to see Mr Banks later this afternoon. Should I give him your regards?"

Mary blinked repeatedly, her mind processing the best form of words for her reply. "I imagine that would be the Christian thing to do. But, Reverend, should you not be observing the Sabbath?"

"I think the Good Lord will allow me to visit the sick bed of a young man electrocuted on the altar steps."

Mrs Meadows's brows knitted across her forehead. I sensed she wanted to say something else. Something that troubled her. But her lips remained shut tight.

"I'll pass on your regards?" My voice lilted, hoping to get a response.

The balls of her eyes flitted under her lids. Water, it seems, was required to lubricate her thoughts. Tears bubbled along her lower lashes. I squeezed her hands firmly, and the pressure of my touch pushed her emotions free of their banks.

"The truth is, Reverend Ward, Jake didn't come home last night." At that moment, the only reason Mary remained standing was the fact that my hands held hers in such a strong vice-like grip.

I freed one hand to reach under her elbow, taking on her full weight as I steered her back into the church. "Mary, please, come back to the vestry with me. Let me help you."

She walked with me down the centre aisle, about a quarter-way down, Mary stopped. She reached out to the back of a pew and braced herself against it. Then, a few beats later, with a single deep breath, the familiar stoic Brown Owl returned. "Tsk. No need to tarry on my behalf, Reverend. Don't know what came over me." She looked back towards a group of stragglers milling at the entrance, catching up on the latest gossip before heading towards the church hall for mulled wine and mince pies. "Your flock is waiting. I'd better get home, anyway. Just one thing." She straightened her scarf and readjusted her spectacles, using the moment to pivot the conversation. "Do you know who won the cake bake? "

***

"Cake Bake? Cake Bake? Give me the challenge of helping inner city youth any day over dealing with middle-England parochial pettiness." I muttered under my breath as I removed my stole in the vestry. "Her son didn't come home!" I wanted to swear but chose to call on the Boss for help instead. "Heavenly Father, give me strength!"

"Are you okay?" Familiar arms wrapped around my waist. "You know, talking to yourself is a bad sign."

I crossed my arms and drew my future husband closer. "Jake Meadows is still missing. He vanished around the time Simon Banks was electrocuted."

Lawrence nuzzled the nape of my neck. "Do you think he had something to do with it?"

If only my gifts boosted analytical thought.

"His absence would suggest he's involved. It could just be a coincidence."

"A pretty suspicious one, if you ask me." Lawrence's body wrapped around me, warming away my concerns. "You know, this time next week I won't be sneaking in to cuddle my fiancée, but will be ravishing my new bride."

"In the vestry of St. Bridget's. I'm sure that's breaking about twelve different commandments." I pivoted to face my beau.

"I'll bow to your greater ecumenical knowledge, but I thought there were only ten." He bowed down and tickled my lips with his.

I reluctantly pushed him away. "Not here. Not now."

He swooped down for one last peck. "Okay, but just so you know. Next week, you will be bound to love, honour, and obey." His eyes flashed with mischief.

I patted his chest. "I'm certain I asked Bishop Marshall to take the 'obey' bit out."

"And maybe I told him to put it back in." He grinned. "Not that I believe for one second you will ever do anything I say."

"Try me?" I taunted, as I lifted the purple chasuble over my head.

"Okay. I forbid you from taking the ferry to the mainland to visit Simon Banks in hospital. Instead, you will come to have Sunday lunch at my mother's."

"Ouch, you've got me!" I bowed to his superior gameplay. "You hit me with a double whammy. You *know* I'm catching that ferry."

Lawrence caught my hair with his right hand and pulled his face down to mine. "That is why I love you. And, Pixley bonus, I'll get second helpings of roast lamb with creamy mashed potatoes. Hmm, tasty..."

The perfect romantic end to our conversation would have been a long, lingering kiss to carry through the rest of the day's activities, but our lips barely touched before there was a knock at the vestry door.

A flushed school secretary followed the knock into the room. "Reverend. Headmaster. I'm terribly sorry. I was waiting in the hall, but, well, I need to get back to put on Stan's lunch."

"Audrey, of course, we were just..." Audrey Matthews knew exactly what she had interrupted. I scanned her face for the look of disapproval, but found only one of concern. "I'm sorry. How can I help you?"

Lawrence bowed his exit, and Audrey sat down on a nearby chair. "I know who tried to kill Mr Banks."

Paper Chains

"**I**'m sorry. Did you say you know who hurt Mr Banks?"

Audrey nodded. "I had slipped back to the school to get some more paper for the stall." One of the many tables featured a "make your own traditional paper chain" stand. People bought ten strips of coloured sticky paper for 10p a pop to make links for the paper chain that would wrap around the Christmas tree in the church. To be honest, I paid little attention to who was running it. *Well, it wasn't selling jars of jam or sticky doughnuts.*

"Ah, you were running the paper chain stand. Sorry, I didn't get that far around the hall —"

"Well, we were stuck in the far corner. Still, we had quite a brisk trade. Raised a hundred odd pounds. Not bad for some scraps of craft paper that were heading to the recycling bin anyway."

I pulled across another chair and placed my hand on Audrey's leg. She was finding it difficult to name what or whom she had seen. "That is remarkable. So, you were heading to the school..."

"No, it was on my way back. There was a gust of wind, you see. I snatched some of the paper out of the box. A few sheets landed on one of the tombstones, and I clambered over to get it. Had to shoo off some of those darn cats before they used it as a litter tray. I heard the screams from the hall. Must have been when the lights went out. So, I looked up, and that's when I saw them."

"Them?"

"Yes. Jake Meadows and Orla Kerrigan. I couldn't hear what they were saying, but Jake ran off down Back Lane. He looked as white as a sheet, you know? And I lost sight of Orla, but I guess she went back inside, because it was her who raised the alarm, wasn't it?"

"Yes, it was. So, Jake was there when the lights went out."

"He looked so scared. I guess he didn't mean for anyone to get hurt. I knew him when he was a pupil at the primary school. He was always such a lovely boy. There's no way he meant any harm, Reverend Ward. Do you think I should tell the police?"

One thing I learned this past year on Wesberrey was that Audrey was a fierce defender of the men in her life. And this she-wolf energy was permeating through every cell in her body. There was a conflict raging inside her. If Jake had hurt Simon, then it was her duty to tell the authorities, but Jake was one of her own. Simon Banks was an outsider.

"Audrey, you know it's the right thing to do." I shifted my hand from her thigh to calm her nervous fingers, wary of upsetting her further. "Why don't we tell Inspector Lovington together?"

She snatched her hand away. "I don't need your help! I'm perfectly capable of talking to the police myself."

"Of course, I didn't mean to suggest —"

Audrey mellowed. "No, sorry, Reverend, I know you meant well. It's just I've known Jake since he was a boy. I can't believe he could do anything like this."

"Maybe he didn't." I ventured. "Perhaps, though, they both saw who did." *And that's why Jake never returned home. What if they saw his own mother tampering with the electrics?*

"I should have told the Inspector when he questioned me back in the hall. I was so confused. You and Phil were giving CPR to Simon when I came back inside. I just snuck back into the hall. I didn't even call for an ambulance or anything. Then I saw Orla was there, and heard she had raised the alarm, so it had to be someone else, right? I mean, why go back in if they had done it?"

"When I was with Phil in the church, did you hear what Orla had to say? How did she seem?"

"Reverend. As I told you, my stand was at the far end. I just scuttled back there as fast as I could and kept my head down. That's awful, isn't it? I mean, my paper chains helped keep some of the younger ones entertained until we could go."

I patted her hand. "And I'm sure there was many a stressed-out parent there who was grateful for that."

We both laughed. A strange series of events to bond over, but I think we may have found peace at last.

***

I hung around long enough to hear Audrey ask to be put through to Inspector Lovington before heading into the hall. The expected horde was thinning out by the time I arrived. My grumbling stomach guided me to what remained of the mince pies.

Fran Fisk was standing by the kitchen hatch. I grabbed two pies, stuffed one in my mouth, and cradled the other in my left hand as I snaked through several sets of animated conversations towards her. "Mrs Fisk, lovely to see you at church this morning. How is your husband this morning?" I swallowed the last bit of savoury filling. "I hope his back's improved."

"Thank you, Vicar. I'm afraid, though, he is quite immobile. Dr Hawthorne said it could be weeks before he's fully up and about again. To be honest, I really should be getting back to him."

"Please, Fran, you need to take him some of the mince pies, at least. I'm sure Barbara will bag some up for you."

"Oh, yes, I will. That's very kind. Have you heard anything about Simon? I mean, you are good friends with Dr Hawthorne and the Inspector. They might have told you. But if you can't tell me, I understand." Mrs Fisk twitched as she spoke. She didn't appear upset, more anxious, jumpy, like she was expecting someone to leap out and surprise her.

"Why would I not be at liberty to tell you?" I felt she was nervous about the answer. "As it stands, there's no further information, but I am heading from here straight to Oysterhaven General. I will let you know if there is any news."

"Thank you. That's most generous of you. I wouldn't want you to go out of your way on my account."

"No trouble at all. And I can help keep Mr Fisk company for a bit if that will help you. It can't be easy with him out of action."

"Not in the run up to Christmas, no. We have the last scout meeting before Christmas to organise. Because Christmas Day is on the Friday, I'm going to suggest we join the Guides at their meeting on Thursday instead. A joint party is more efficient and I hope, given all that has happened, it will put an end to all this rivalry."

"That's sounds like a wonderful idea. If you need me to mediate. I would be happy to do so. Well, like I said, I will pop by later with news of Simon and we can talk then." I guided Fran over to the pies, took down her home address and made good my goodbyes, before sneaking away to take Cilla down to the harbour. *With God's speed, I will make the start of visiting time.*

***

I arrived at the hospital with enough time before the published visiting hour to pop to the League of Friends kiosk to get a paper cup of dishwater pretending to be coffee and a Get Well Soon card. Using a scratchy blue pen taped to a piece of string lying on the reception desk in the foyer, I completed the card, wishing Simon a speedy recovery on behalf of the parish. Ink blotches covered my fingers and the silky white envelope. *It's the thought that counts.*

As it was a Sunday, a skeleton staff ran the administrative areas of the hospital, which meant in practice the security desk near the parking payment machines fielded most enquiries. The queue of visitors like me needing ward directions was several feet deep. It took almost half an hour to reach the counter, but once there, it was a matter of seconds to find out what ward the young Cub Master was on.

Emma, a hygienically scrubbed cherub and uber keen student nurse, offered to take me to Simon's bed. "Mr Banks is very popular today. I took a couple of other visitors down earlier. Strictly, it's only two to a bed, but if you promise not to tell matron, I'm sure it will be fine."

She pulled back the curtain screen to reveal Jake Meadows and Orla Kerrigan.

"Jake!" I gasped.

"Reverend Ward, we can explain."

Simple Simon

"It's all so awful." Orla dabbed away the black mascara rivers from her freckled cheek. "Simon hasn't spoken. He's barely moved."

Jake reached a comforting arm around his girlfriend's shoulders. "The doctor came by earlier, but as we're not relatives, he wouldn't tell us what's going on."

"Do you think they'll tell you?" Orla sniffed. "What with you being a member of the clergy and all?"

Both stared up at me, their heads angling like a pair of cautious kittens. Forlorn eyes pooled wide as saucers, their complexions under the fluorescent lighting gleamed pale as the moon. I felt like I was looking at one of those Dallas Simpson prints from my childhood.

"I will ask, but in exchange, the two of you are going to tell me what you were doing near the graveyard just after the lights went out. And Jake, you're going to tell me why you haven't been home."

They both gauged where each other stood before answering. Orla bobbed her head in agreement and Jake replied. "We'll tell you everything."

My dog collar and vicar's garb open many doors, especially with other caring professionals. It didn't take me long to track down Simon's physician and get an update on his condition. I knew the star-crossed lovers were a potential flight risk, but I had to trust my gut that they would not take my absence as an opportunity to run away.

My instincts were on point. *Or is that en pointe? I never really know the difference.* Either way, they were spot on. Jake and Orla were still exactly where I left them.

"The doctor says they have sedated Simon to make him more comfortable. His burns are quite severe and there are signs of cataracts in his eyes, caused by the shock. He will need an operation in due course. He is probably in a lot of pain and, for the moment, the staff want to keep him comfortable whilst they run more tests and initiate treatment. But his prognosis is good and they believe he will make a full recovery."

"Oh, thank the Lord!" Jake collapsed in his chair. His relief was palpable. "Reverend, can you say a few words?"

I stood between them and took their hands. Both squeezed their eyes shut so tight that I was worried they would also need cataract operations. "Dear Father in Heaven, please look after our friend and colleague, Simon, and help him on his healing journey. Please rest your loving eyes upon your humble servants, Jake and Orla, as they hold their vigil by Simon's bedside. Keep us all safe in your everlasting love. Amen."

"Amen," Jake mumbled.

Orla nodded. Her Catholic upbringing fought against a public amen. "Thank you, Reverend."

"My pleasure. Now, tell me what happened." I cleared a green duffle bag from a faded tapioca-coloured wing-backed chair by Simon's nightstand. "Does this belong to him?" I asked.

"No, well, yes. You see, technically, it's my bag, but I brought him a few things. A new toothbrush, some toothpaste, soap. I picked them up from the store on the way over." Jake wrung his hands together. "Be prepared, that's the Scout motto, right? Though no one could have prepared us for this."

"So, Jake, that's very thoughtful of you. Let's ease ourselves into this, shall we? Where did you sleep last night?"

"On the ferry. Under some tarpaulin. Woke up as we crossed to the mainland. It was still dark. I just slipped out with the other passengers. Though, I will pay my fare, it's just I didn't want anyone to see me and you know, call the police."

"So you have been in Oysterhaven all day?"

"Yes, since before sunrise. Orla came over about an hour ago and we had McDonalds for lunch."

"Very nice." There was something charming about Jake and Orla, though they were both in their twenties they had a naivety which was rare in this modern age. It was very endearing and made it hard to believe they could be behind whatever happened to the comatose man lying in the bed between us. "So, that explains where you were all night, but leaves the question why you felt you had to run and hide."

Orla clasped both hands around Jake's and inhaled deeply. "His mother told him to."

"She did what?" *My 'gast' is well and truly flabbered.* "Mrs Meadows told you to run?" Maybe my approach was too back to front to make any sense of their story. "Let's wheel back a little. What happened at the bazaar?"

"The stall was running out of doughnuts. We had made loads and there were several boxes left in the storeroom, but we hadn't brought them all through to the hall because we were a bit late setting up and Mrs Fisk was getting a little flustered, so we set up with the first few boxes so we'd be ready when the bazaar opened." He stopped to take in a much-needed breath. "Then, when we were running low, Simon and I set off to get more. Mr Fisk followed. I think he wanted to get away from the hubbub for a while."

"And that's when I saw Jake. It's my fault." Orla began to cry again. "I waved him over, and we snuck off to the back gate."

Jake's teeth grated, and the muscles in the square of his jaw pulsed. "Yes, and I guess Simon must have gone looking for me, or something because he left the storeroom at some point and ended up in the church by the tree. Unconscious."

"Reverend Ward, we have no idea what happened. We were round back and there was this loud bang and the lights went out. We ran inside the church because that was where the crashing sound came from and saw Simon lying there. As we circled back to the hall, Mrs Meadows was right there. Like lurking in the shadows. She scared me half to death."

"I told my mother Simon looked dead, and she told me to run. Like she told us both to shoo, like don't look back. And that she would sort everything."

"But when we got outside, I couldn't. I mean, we had to get an ambulance or something." Orla grew more distraught with each word she uttered. "So I went back into the hall."

"And raised the alarm. Yes, I was there. Mr Fisk had thrown his back, bringing in the boxes, poor man."

"Oh, no!" Jake looked guiltily at Orla. "He wouldn't have gotten hurt if I had been there to help." He edged his chair away and turned his back on his girlfriend. "Mother was right. See what you have done. I should have nothing to do with you. You lead me astray."

"Jake, none of this is Orla's fault, or yours, either, from what you've said." His hissy fit made me understand how immature their relationship was, or at least, how domineering Mrs Meadows was with her son. "Orla came back. You still ran off. Why was that?"

"Because my mother told me to."

"You didn't see her, Reverend. She was so angry." Orla nudged Jake's leg with her knee. He continued to block her, his folded arms forming an impenetrable wall to his heart. Thoughts of hurt and betrayal bounced around her face. "You don't suppose she did it, do you, Reverend?"

"Why on earth would she want to harm Simon?" I patted the edge of his mattress. The strong, vibrant Cub Master looked so vulnerable beneath all the tubes and monitors.

"I don't know." Orla shrugged. "But she was right there. Why? What was she doing back there?"

This accusation was the final straw for Jake. He stood up and strode to the end of the bed, grinding his fist into the palm of his other hand. "So now you are blaming my mother. She was trying to protect us!"

"From what?" Orla screamed back. "We didn't do anything!"

"But she thought we did. Why else would we be sneaking around?"

"We were sneaking around because you're too much of a baby to tell that witch about us." Orla reached under the bed and grabbed her handbag. "I've had enough of this. I love you, Jake Meadows, but my mother taught me better than to waste my life on a stupid man-child."

She pushed past him and ran out of the ward. Even though she didn't look back, I knew she had tears in her eyes.

"Do you want to go after her? I can stay with Simon."

"No, Reverend." He paused. "There's a chapel here, isn't there?"

"Yes, of course. I think it's on the ground floor." I believe we are all served by speaking to the big guy, but not if it's a way of avoiding what has to be done. "Do you love her?" I asked.

"Yes, I think so."

"Then, go. God helps those who help themselves, remember?"

Jake Meadows, tired, broken-hearted, and probably still thawing out from a night on-board the ferry, stood motionless at the end of the bed. "But what if she's right? What if my mother did this terrible thing?"

What a Pleasant Surprise!

I stayed with Jake by Simon's bedside until visiting hours ended. The nurses came by a few times to check his vitals, but Simon remained unconscious throughout. Jake talked about his friend and how he admired him.

"He has a natural gift with the children, you know. That's why they all prefer Cubs and Beavers to Brownies. I've tried to explain that to my mother. Make her see that the young girls aren't interested in embroidery and scrapbooking. Well, some of them are, of course. Even some of the boys would be, I guess. Simon is fun to be around. He makes them laugh."

"Well, he has quite the fan club. I hear he's quite the heartthrob amongst the girls."

Jake's lips curled. "He would find that hysterical. You know he's gay, right?"

"I didn't." *Not that it matters.* The irony. "Did you know Mrs Whittaker is convinced Orla had eyes for Simon, not you?"

Jake smiled down at his friend. "Well, who wouldn't pick him over me?"

I think I can rule out jealousy as a motive. Jake did not hurt his friend.

"You should message her. Say you're sorry."

"I will. Reverend, can I ask you a huge favour?"

"Of course, fire away."

"Will you give me a lift back on your scooter?"

***

Bob McGuire met us at the ferry port, and true to his word, Jake paid for two tickets. He may be a Mummy's boy, but he was an honest man.

"Jake, just one more question. When you ran, why didn't you take the next ferry out? They would still have been sailing at that time."

"I ran to the far side of the island first. Which was really stupid. I mean, where was I planning to go from there? Ride into the sunset on the back of a nearby seal? I circled back and reached the end of Back Lane in time to see the helicopter take Simon away. I moved slowly. Hid behind fences and walls in case the police spotted me. By the time I got to the harbour, it was too late, and I was so tired. I just wanted a safe place to sleep."

"Okay, that makes sense. And you didn't think of going to Orla's, or back home?"

"That's the first place they would look. I'm not a complete idiot!"

No, dear boy, you are not.

I offered to take him all the way to his mother's house, but he wanted to walk. To clear his head, he said. Tempting as it was to rush ahead and interrogate Mary Meadows about her reasons for telling her son to dash off into the night, I chose to heed her words about the sabbath instead. I had a busy week ahead of me, full of Christmas services and wedding plans. Simon Banks was alive, and everything else could wait.

***

The delicate aroma of toasted chestnuts greeted me as I wheeled Cilla up the path to the vicarage. Someone has been cooking. My nose led me merrily through the front door, down the hall and into the kitchen where Tilly, Luke, Freya, and Dominic were all busy putting the finishing touches to an epic vegetarian roast dinner.

The table groaned under servings of golden parsnips, crispy potatoes, fresh green vegetables, carrots, field mushrooms, caramelised onions and ramekins of cranberry sauce. Freya lifted an oval serving plate over the heads of my other guests and placed a glorious nut roast in the centre.

My copper-topped niece looked up as I entered. "Hope you don't mind, but we thought you might be hungry."

She beamed.

They all did.

My heart pumped so hard it filled my chest. There was nothing I could do but grin like the Cheshire Cat from ear-to-ear. These were my children. I may not have given birth to them, but if this is the pride a mother feels, then they have experienced the ultimate joy of divine love. I cannot imagine any greater force in the universe.

"Mind? Of course not. I'm famished."

Luke pulled out a chair at the end of the table for me to sit at. "Everyone else is around Aunt Pam's. We thought we would surprise you."

"Surprise!" sniggered Dominic. "There's apple crumble for dessert. I think Luke nicked it from D and V. And vegan custard. Who knew there even was such a thing?"

Freya ruffled his brown locks. "Rosie will have you converted before you know it." She sat down at the opposite end of the table. "Right, let's tuck in."

Everyone leapt into the feast before us. I raised my hand. "Do you mind if I say grace first?"

There followed an awkward pause. Hands cupping serving bowls of vegetables froze across the table. Darting eyes, the only visible movement in this comedic freeze-frame. I summoned all my wizarding powers to wave their arms down again. Unburdened hands shrank back to the table's edge, where they linked instead for prayer. *They're so cute!*

"Thank you. I'll keep it brief." I smiled. "Dear Lord, we gather here as witnesses to your gracious love and earthly bounty. For the food we are about to receive, we are truly grateful." They mumbled words, offering variations on the traditional 'Amen' and sat patiently for my command. "Okay, that's it. Eat!"

It truly was a magnificent spread. I was both impressed and honoured.

Luke passed me the roasted parsnips. "So, what do you think they are talking about at Pam's? Byron's probably hiding out in his shed, bless him."

"Why we're here, not there." Freya laughed. "But I wanted to spend some time with Dom, and my favourite aunt, of course. And Mum needs more alone time with Clara and Phoebe. They have a lot of catching up to do."

"What do they think of the Baron?" I asked.

"Same as they think about all Mum's boyfriends. He's very handsome. They always are. He's besotted with her. They always are."

Luke stuffed a mushroom in his mouth and swallowed hard, almost choking in the process. "But this one's a keeper, right?"

"Luke, I agree. I think this one is." I cornered off a mouthful of nut roast with my fork. "I guess with all things, time will tell. But he's a baron, right?"

"Son of a baronet." Freya corrected me. "He's invited us all to his estate to ring in the New Year. And I haven't packed my ballgown!"

Dominic slid up next to his girlfriend. "I have a tux. Can you take a plus one?"

She swooped in to plant a kiss on the end of his nose. "Can't see how he can say no if you have a tuxedo."

I spotted Luke gazing over to Tilly from under his curly fringe. At that moment, I realised I was the only one at the table with straight hair. *I'm surrounded by Cabbage Patch kids.*

Tilly took advantage of the lull in the conversation to ask about Simon. "What's the news on the Cub leader?"

"He's going to be okay, but he has a long way to go." *Hmm, this nut roast is delicious.* "All I know is that it wasn't Jake Meadows, or Orla Kerrigan, who tampered with the Christmas lights."

"My money's on Jake's mother. Orla is always moaning about her when she pops into the Cat and Fiddle." Tilly stabbed at a carrot. "Some people are so narrow-minded."

I had my own suspicions about Mary myself, but I couldn't see what her motive could be. "My question is why? What had Simon Banks done to Mrs Meadows to cause her to act like that?"

Tilly batted my words back with the end of her fork. "Just because? She's lonely. Miserable. Losing her status. Feels threatened. Simon is taking her son away from her. If she knew about Orla, we would be looking at two dead bodies."

Luke gulped down a mouthful of apple juice. *That boy needs to learn how to eat more slowly.* "Simon isn't dead."

"Not from the want of trying. He's very lucky."

Very lucky indeed.

As grateful as I was for the company of these young people and the beautiful food they had prepared, my energy stores needed to be replaced with more than a slice of apple crumble. With a second bowl, washed down with a soothing cup of tea, I made my excuses and left them to a late evening of smooching over the washing up. I retired to my bed and fell asleep. A comforting lullaby of sweet nothings swirled into my dreams from the floor below as the party dispersed into the night. The last thing I heard was Tilly calling in Hugo from his night-time wander.

I am very lucky too.

Prepare To Dye

Peppered by a series of thunderstorms and heavy downpours, the next two days flew by in a squall of parish commitments and meetings. I had heard from Zuzu that Jake had turned himself into the police for questioning. Dave released him a few hours later without charge. News from Oysterhaven General was that Simon Banks was showing steady improvement, but was still unconscious. There was still no word on Muriel.

To be honest, with my heavy work schedule and wedding preparations, I had given little thought to either Muriel or Simon. I trusted Dave was investigating all possible avenues. It was his job to track down criminals, not mine. Mine was to visit the sick and housebound and bring them Christmas cheer on these cold, wet days, in between visits to the florists to confirm flower arrangements, further dress fittings with my mother and seating plan discussions for the wedding breakfast in the vestry hall.

The reality was I barely spoke to the rest of my family outside of these last-minute arrangements. They were busy getting to know each other and the island, and that suited me just fine. *Too many cooks and all that.* The upshot was I was totally out of the gossip loop, but I fancied our planned trip to the hairdressers would change all that.

Zuzu had booked out the salon for the whole day. A treat of primping and preening awaited us all. I'm not a huge fan of pampering or coiffuring, I am very low maintenance, but even I could appreciate the need to look a tad more polished on my wedding day. And so it was that around nine o'clock on Wednesday morning, I left Tilly filling in her online university application form and strolled down, umbrella in hand, to my appointment at the island's most popular stylists, well, the only stylists, Scissor Sisters.

Avril and Verity greeted me with matching leather pencil skirts and leopard-skin tops. Avril, voluptuous in a shade of electric blue and her twin in a figure-hugging bright pink. They wore acrylic nails to match.

"Reverend Ward! How's the blushing bride, then?" Verity took my coat and ushered me past the reception desk. "Avril and I were wondering if you wanted to spice up your colour. Just a few gold highlights. Your dress is ivory, I believe. Would work so well with your complexion."

"Yes, no secrets around here, eh?" I blushed. "Vintage lace. I'm not sure about highlights."

The sisters' senior stylist, Dwayne, swung an empty black leather chair around to meet me. "Girl, were we wrong about the bob or the latte?" I stared at him, open-mouthed. *I am fond of my hair the way it is.* "Babe, I think the words 'Dwayne, you're a genius,' are what you are searching for." He clicked his fingers in front of my face. "Are you doing your own make-up? Please say no."

"Er, no?" I replied as he pushed me down in to the chair and swivelled me around to face the mirror. It was only then that I noticed my sisters were already sitting on either side.

Zuzu waved her hand in protest at the thought of me being left to my own devices. "Don't you worry your pretty head, Dwayne darling, I have that all under control. Verity, highlight away. Let me have a look at the colour charts." My sister dropped her hand and tapped her nails on the counter between us. "Jessie, let them do their thing. They don't come into your church and tell you how to pray. This is their cathedral. Sit back and allow."

My other sister, Rosie, was much more game than I. "Man, I needed this. The cafe is hard work. A whole day of TLC is just what the doctor ordered. Is Sam joining us later?"

I looked around. "She said she was coming. So, what's the plan, hair first?"

Avril bowed in between us. "Yes, then manicure, pedicure, lunch, and a massage. We'll finish with a seaweed facial."

"A massage? I didn't know you did those?"

"Oh, it's new. Verity and I took on a masseuse last month. Kylie has a gift. She's proving very popular. Antipodean. We have a room out back. Outback? Did you see what I did there?"

Verity giggled politely at her sister's little joke. "You'll love what we've done with the room. Very Zen."

"Yeah, comes with a built in waterfall, thanks to the rain." Dwayne ran the metal end of a black plastic comb through my hair, lifting out sections and tutting. "But don't worry, I'm sure the roof won't cave in on you." *Good to know.* "Are you wearing a veil? You should have brought it with you."

"Mum said she'll bring it." I turned to Zuzu. "They are coming, right?"

"Of course, Jessie. Relax. We have staggered appointments. They'll be here soon, weather permitting. And we'll get to see the veil!" She clapped. "You know, girls, she won't let us see the dress?" My older sister was so excited, anyone would think she was getting married.

An hour and a bit later, as promised, Mum arrived with my aunts Pam and Cindy. They were all slightly wind blown. The heavens had opened as they rounded onto Market Square. They barely had time to shake the water off their umbrellas before Dwayne whisked my veil from my mother's hand and placed it on top of my head.

He stood back to admire his handiwork. Avril and Verity linked their arms around his tie-dyed waist. Their verdict?

"Sheer perfection!"

"Darling, what did I say?"

"You're a genius. Inspired!"

I could see in the mirror's reflection my mother beating her swollen, if damp, chest with pride. My aunts squeezing her on both sides. I refocused. *I hate looking at myself.* My gaze shifted from the background to my own reflection.

Wow!

My cheeks flushed. My eyes sparkled.

It's so pretty!

I'm pretty.

"Thank you."

Dwayne leaned his face in next to mine, his hands on both my shoulders. "You're welcome, my darling. Now, get out of my chair. Next!"

***

Lunch, of course, was courtesy of Dungeons and Vegans. I was desperate to tuck in straight away, but my freshly painted nails were still wet. Zuzu, obviously more accustomed to operating with manicured talons, used a toothpick to skewer an olive and popped it into her mouth. She was about to go in for a second one when her phone rang. Skilfully picking her mobile up from the table with the pads of her fingertips, she swiped to answer and balanced it close to her ear.

"It's Dave." she mouthed. Several 'ums' and 'ahhs' later, she placed the phone back on the table. "He's heading to Oysterhaven. They've found a body near the cottage."

The salon took a collective sharp intake of breath. We all thought the worst, only Cindy voiced it.

"Muriel?"

The Charmed sisters, all three now camped in a row facing the mirrors, as it was their turn to be coiffed, stretched out their hands, and closed their eyes. If Muriel had passed on, they would find her.

I'm not sure what Avril, Verity or Dwayne made of all this, but they continued to snip and curl away, seemingly oblivious to the witchy goings on in front of them. They were in the zone.

The anticipation set my stomach rumbling. *How can I be hungry at a time like this? My nails must be dry now.* My ravenous eyes spotted a vegan sausage roll with my name on it and I swooped in. Sated, for now, I waved my greasy fingers at my sisters. "Come on. Maybe they don't have enough power. Let's join hands."

Zuzu and Rosie didn't need to be asked twice. "What do we do?" Rosie asked as she licked stray salsa from the edge of her lip.

Zuzu grabbed her hand. "Just close your eyes and think of Muriel. Then we just say what we see."

What we saw was nothing.

"She's not dead." Cindy called over from the mirrors. With relief, we all dropped out.

Rosie took a breadstick and went in for more of the tangy tomato dip. "So, whose body is it?"

"Let's not get ahead of ourselves." Seconds before a hummus covered cracker stopped up my mouth. "Just because we can't connect with her spirit doesn't mean it isn't her."

"I don't understand why we didn't see anything." Zuzu brushed some crumbs from her chest. "I mean, you and I picked up the Norma Jean that time. And back at the cottage, we all saw the nun. Seems strange to me we can't see a thing now."

"Do you think this has something to do with Sister Elizabeth? Maybe she's interfering with the signal, or something? I've literally no idea how any of this stuff works." Rosie was right. None of us knew what was going on. If the nun could transport me to another dimension and make me imagine I was being dragged by hellhounds, perhaps she could block out Muriel's cries for help from beyond the grave.

A door behind us creaked opened, and a soft Australian voice called over to us. "Hi there, I think I've fixed the leak. Who's first for a massage?"

That must be Kylie.

O, Tannenbaum

"**H**ope you don't mind, Vicar, but I've taken the liberty of decorating the tree with a new set of lights."

I walked into the church to find Phil and Barbara putting the finishing touches to the tree for that evening's candlelight carol service. "Why would I mind? I hope you kept the receipt."

"Of course. Beautiful Babs here has already paid me back through petty cash."

Babs blushed. *It is lovely to see them flirting with each other as they did when we first met.* "We have another question, though, about the topper. Should it be the star or the angel?"

"Dare I ask who sold the most doughnuts?"

"Well, that's the problem. With all the drama and confusion on Saturday, no one totalled up the takings. They were all just thrown into a cash box and locked away in the safe overnight. We have a total amount of the whole bazaar but can't tell which stall did best."

"Then, in the circumstances, we should put up the star. Surely no one would object to that with Simon Banks spending his Christmas in a hospital bed." My favourite couple nodded in agreement. "That's decided then. Hopefully, it will serve as a reminder to people what Christmas is really about."

Phil went back to the storeroom to fetch the notorious decoration, leaving his wife and me to put out the candles. "I can think of a couple of women who won't be happy with our decision." Barbara sighed.

"To be honest, I think the Scouts were winning anyway. Their doughnuts were much nicer."

"You don't think that's why she did it?" Barbara twiddled with a tiny Christmas stocking dangling from her right ear.

I stopped at the end of the pew. "Why who did what?"

"Why did Mary Meadows try to light up Mr Banks? If it wasn't Jake, it had to be her. I know the police think as much. Stanley Matthews said he saw her being taken away by Inspector Lovington yesterday afternoon for a chat just before the market closed. Stan says he took her into the Guildhall, and they didn't come back out for a good hour. All the stalls were packed up by then."

"Hmm, that's a good idea, using the old Guildhall as a makeshift interrogation room. We should have thought of that before." My mind whirled with the proposition that Mary Meadows was Dave's prime suspect. Was that why she told Jake to run? Did that explain her anxious behaviour at church? If so, did she really try to kill him over a Christmas tree topper? And why didn't Dave tell us he had her in his sights? *I guess, because it's none of our business!*

"Reverend, did you hear me? The Inspector interviewed Brown Owl. Why would he do that if she's not a suspect?"

"I don't know. Perhaps he was simply trying to corroborate Jake's story." I muttered, my mind completely absent as I wandered down the next aisle, dropping candles onto the bench below. "Jake's testimony places his mother close to the scene of the crime. But if she had gone to the toilets to compose herself, that's exactly where I would expect to find her."

"Reverend, you don't think she did it then?" Barbara walked towards me on along the adjacent pew.

"I guess anyone is capable of anything. I still don't see what she had against Simon, though." *If she had tried to kill Orla, it would make more sense.* "Could she really have not known about Jake and Orla's affair?"

"In my experience, people see only what they want to see. Mary Meadows would have a hard time seeing any other woman in her son's life, if you ask me."

"Exactly, but what if she knew, but thought Orla was cheating on Jake… That could be motive enough."

Candle boxes empty, we stood, pensively, in the centre aisle and stared at the pine tree. Phil was climbing a stepladder with the star ornament gripped between his teeth. Love for her man oozed out of Barbara's every pore. Her admiration and devotion were without question.

"You have a good man there, Barbara."

"Oh, I know, Reverend. I love the bones of the man and that's a fact. Just like you and the headmaster, eh?" She chuckled. "We're truly blessed, aren't we? To have found our true loves so late in life. Just goes to show. It's never too late."

Do I love the bones of Lawrence?

I hesitated.

Why did I hesitate?

Jess, stop it! You love Lawrence. You do. This is just pre-wedding jitters. There's a lot going on.

But do I love the bones of the man? What a bizarre expression? But do I?

"Is it on straight?" Phil's cockney baritone snapped me out of the well of doubt I was spiralling into.

Jess! Focus. You're to be wed in three days' time. Doubting Thomas had more faith in Christ's resurrection than you have in — well, let's be honest whilst I'm talking to myself — anything!

I clapped my approval for the star's alignment, more to snap myself out of my destructive musings than as a sign of excitement. *I will have a strong word with myself later.*

"Phil, it's perfect." My words came out in a visual stream. The temperature had dropped considerably. "I say, we head into the hall and put the kettle on. The choir will be here to set up in just over an hour."

"Now you're talking, Reverend." Barbara signalled for Phil to join us. "By the way, I meant to say something earlier. I really like what you've done with your hair."

***

Maybe it was the milky tea. Maybe it was my post-lunch massage. Maybe it was pure exhaustion — it had been a busy week. Maybe it was all or none of the above. One thing was for sure. It was increasingly difficult to hide my cavernous yawns behind my empty mug.

I needed to move. Growing older, I have noticed that once you stop, decades of sleep deprivation catch up and try to drag you into an eternal slumber — or at the very least, a short nap. And, I didn't have time for that. Phil and Barbara, content all the necessary preparations were done, were busy brewing a second pot, which I declined.

"Guys, if it's all the same with you, I'm going to head to the vestry and get myself ready for the carol service."

Barbara waved from the kitchen. "You do what you have to do, Reverend. We'll be along later."

Alone in the panelled antechamber, my doubts crashed back like storm waves off the headland by Wesberrey's lighthouse. I have always been the cautious one. Zuzu had spent her life throwing caution to the four winds before we had the faintest idea we could summon them. Both she and Rosie had accepted our pagan past and associated powers more readily than I had done.

Yes, it was a question of faith, but it ran deeper. Much deeper. Rosie came to the island destitute and heartbroken and has set up a successful new business. *Strike that, several businesses.* She had even bounced back from further betrayal like the trooper she is. Whereas I was questioning everything. That was my way and until now, it had served me well.

Questioning has led me to my vocation. I loved being an Anglican vicar. I had enjoyed acting, but in my heart, I knew it was a fleeting fancy. The accident merely sped up the process. My career had brought me back home, but I had my doubts before I came here. I was wrong about that. I was wrong about so many things. *How can I be sure I am right about Lawrence?*

Remember, you almost left. I did. My first week here, I was going to resign. I was wrong about that as well. *I am happy here. Happier than I have ever been.*

The people I love most in the world are here. My family, my best friends. And Lawrence?

Yes. Yes. YES!

My feet danced as I layered on my robes. I swirled around the vestry to my own song. The love of a thousand lives.

Yes, it is quick. So what? Yes, we are older. Who cares? Yes. Yes. YES!

I slumped into an oak carver chair by the mahogany dresser. My still bruised behind found comfort in its velvet padded cushion. *Jess Ward, sometimes you ask too many questions for your own good. Just accept. Stop over-thinking.*

I paused to catch my breath. People would be filing into the church soon. Lawrence would be there soon setting up. I glanced at the wall clock. *No, still plenty of time. Just a quick word with the Big Boss.*

***

150

Some people would find an empty church an eery place, but I have always relished having the place to myself. The yellow glow of the advent candles and the new Christmas lights flickered ahead as I walked through the north transept into the chancel, calling me to my special place.

I had turned left to the altar steps, past the tree, when everything save the advent crown plunged in to darkness. Behind me, a rustling of branches and a loud creaking sound heralded a crushing pressure on my back, forcing me down onto the cold marble before me.

I threw out my hands to cushion the fall, but the force pinned me down beneath it. Pine needles pricked my skin. Somewhere to my side, I could make out footsteps scurrying away. They sounded like heels on the stone floor. *A woman?*

When Trees Attack!

I crawled down the steps, freeing myself from the Norwegian spruce, and sat for a few moments on the bottom step. *Did I trip on the wire and yank out the lights, pulling the tree down on top of me? Of course not. Jess, you heard the footsteps. Someone did this and ran off.*

The church lights came on. Phil and Barbara hurried toward me. My eyes struggled to adjust to the glare as I staggered back up the steps towards the plug socket. The cable lay coiled by the wall and underneath the wire was a red metal object. *A Swiss army knife! Ginny!*

My snowy-haired verger got to me first. "Vicar! Are you okay? We heard the most awful crash."

"Yes, Phil, thank you. I'm a little shaken. Not every day a tree attacks me on the altar steps." I laughed. "There are needles lodged everywhere, but I'm fine." I needed to think fast. Hundreds of carollers would be here soon. "Barbara, can you fetch me a pair of the blue disposable gloves we keep in the kitchen and one of those clear lunch bags? There's some evidence here Dave, I mean Inspector Lovington, might want to dust for prints."

Barbara pivoted on her heels like a flamenco dancer and dashed back into the hall. I asked Phil to make sure that no one else came in until we had made the area secure. I thought about running after the Girl Guide leader, but this was an island and the last ferry had gone for the night. *Where would she go? She came back to the scene of the crime to strike again. She's not about to disappear. Anyway, Wesberrey is her home.*

Barbara came back with more than gloves and a plastic bag.

"Lawrence!" I have never been more pleased to see him.

"Jess, what on earth happened?" He stretched out his arms for a hug. I weaved out of reach.

"I'll tell you in a bit. For now, can you help Phil get the tree back up?" I took the latex gloves and shook them. "Oh, and by the way, I love you very, very much."

Refocusing, I pulled one half of the pair over my right hand and then did the same with my left. Nudging the cable aside with my toe, I bent down and picked up the knife between my middle finger and thumb and popped it into the bag. "Barbara, we need to put this somewhere safe. There's the perfect cupboard in the vestry. The key's in my desk drawer. I need to get these needles out of my hair. The rest of the congregation will be here soon."

"You can't be going to host the carol concert after the fright you've had."

"Nonsense, Barbara. The show must go on. People have dragged themselves out on this windy, wet night to sing and get their hands covered in burning drops of wax. Why would we want to deny them that seasonal pleasure, eh?"

"Well, if you put it like that. I'll go get you a hairbrush."

Moments later and order restored, we opened the doors. Parishioners, many I hadn't seen all year, poured in, filling the seats in family groupings, leaving awkward gaps in the centre for late comers to clamber into.

Children in the choir waved at their proud parents as they skipped across the south transept where Lawrence was setting up his accordion.

Rosemary was off duty this evening, so no organ music. *Every cloud has a silver lining, and all that jazz - no one can ever keep in time with the piped music anyway.* My parish treasurer still joined us for the concert, ready to sing along in her best soprano voice. Soon the church was full of people keen to get into the festive spirit.

I sat in a chair in the apse, watching and waiting. My gut told me Ginny Whitaker would join us. Her absence at such an important community event as the annual carol service would cause suspicion. My guess was that in her haste she would either not have realised she had left a clue behind, or if she knew, would look for an opportunity to retrieve it.

What I didn't know was why. Why had she tried to attack me with a spruce tree? Why had she tried to kill Simon Banks?

While brushing my hair, I called Dave to give him an update. He was dining with my sister and her three grown-up daughters and, from the tone of his voice, seemed grateful for a reason to excuse himself. If my instincts were right, he would find Miss Whitaker here this evening, and I granted him permission to use the vestry to interview her.

I spotted Mary Meadows in the second row closest to the choir with her son. Orla sat next to Jake, leaning over and whispering in his ear. Their public display of affection caused a smile to curl across my lips. As I watched, they all budged up a spot to let in the last member of their party — Ginny Whitaker. *I knew it! Maybe I'm better at this psychic stuff than I thought.*

A quick nod across to my fiancé, and the opening chords of *O Come All Ye Faithful* floated up into the eaves. I took my spot at the pulpit and the service began. During *Once in Royal David's City,* Akela, a.k.a. Frances Fisk, snuck in quietly at the back. She was alone. Frank must still be out of action. *Poor man.*

Keeping a weather eye on my tree-toppling quarry, I led the service of short readings and anticipatory prayer. The carols followed one after the other. The traditional canon is sung year after year, generation after generation within these stone walls and in Christian gatherings the world over. United in faith and love.

"Yet in thy dark streets shineth, the everlasting light The hopes and fears of all the years are met in thee tonight."

The dying chords of *O Little Town of Bethlehem* announced it was time to light our candles. When I received the signal that we were ready from Phil, I would switch off all the overhead lighting and St Bridget's would become a Christmas grotto.

Though I wished Dave was here to keep Ms Whitaker under surveillance as we set about plunging the church into near darkness, we couldn't delay. It was vital to carry on as normal. *I don't think Ginny suspects anything.*

"If everyone can stand, we will conduct the rest of the service in candlelight. Please be careful not to catch the flames in people's hair and clothing. And watch for dripping wax. Whilst we do this, let us sing *Jog Along Little Donkey to Bethlehem*. The youngest members of the choir particularly love this one."

Barbara and Phil lit tapers from the advent crown and passed down the centre aisle, lighting the first candle in each row. The flames played tag across the pews. I walked to the side to turn off the overhead lights and waited. Dave appeared under the porch arch just as I flipped the switch.

The hymns continued. Wicks blackened. White molten blobs fell onto the cardboard circles beneath. I took myself a candle and walked around the church, singing every festive note with gusto and smiling to everyone as I passed them by.

When I reached the inspector, I pointed out where Ginny was standing. We were quite a team. I didn't need to speak a word for him to know what to do next. As I continued to head in her direction and the inspector followed close behind.

I neared the choir and paused at the end of the pew to shake Ginny's hand. She looked askance, then cast a side eye to the inspector by my side. Her bottom lip trembled so slightly, I thought it may have been a trick of the flickering candle in her hand, but her eyes signalled her resignation. With a genteel nod, she stepped out of the pew and walked with Dave back up the side aisle and out through the side porch.

I breezed back to the pulpit and continued the service as if nothing had happened. *In the legendary words of the A team's John Hannibal' Smith - I love it when a plan comes together.*

"Dearly Beloved, what a wonderful sight. All of us joined here this evening to celebrate in song the birth of our Saviour, Jesus Christ. Let us go forth into the night with our final hymn. *Ding, Dong Merrily on High* and I urge you all to really go for the Glorias!"

Devious Doughnuts

Helpful Girl Guides collected spent candles at the exit, whilst their leader answered police questions in the vestry. Gate-crashing an interrogation is not the normal way to end a carol concert, but I had to disrobe. *And it's my vestry.*

I knocked on the door. "Sorry, Inspector, I'm afraid I need to come in."

Ginny Whitaker perched on the carver chair I had rested on earlier. Her indignant countenance suggested that she considered the inspector's line of questioning to be banal and bordering on the moronic. "Reverend Ward, at last we might have some sort of intelligent conversation."

Dave's eye twitched in response. "Miss Whitaker, you don't seem to appreciate the seriousness of this situation. I have arrested you for attempted murder."

"Inspector Lovington, I am well aware of that fact. I believe that my behaviour so far has been exemplary. I have provided succinct and pertinent answers to your asinine questions to the best of my ability. The fact is, you have no evidence."

"That is where you are greatly mistaken, Miss Whitaker. Reverend Ward, where have you put the weapon?"

Ginny laughed. "Anyone could have planted my knife at the scene of the crime. Is that all you have?"

I took a small brass key from the desk drawer and unlocked a corner cabinet where Barbara and I had earlier secured the 'weapon'. "One question, Ms Whitaker. How did you know we had a knife? No one said anything about a knife."

Dave picked up on my lead. "There is no way you could have known we had a knife. Your knife. A Swiss army knife. Unless you knew you dropped it by the electrical socket earlier."

"After all, Miss Whitaker, Simon Banks was electrocuted. Only his assailant would know the socket was tampered with using a pen knife." I handed the bag to Dave, who held it above his head to get a better look in the light. "What I don't get, Ginny, is why? Was it to protect Orla? You do know she is seeing Jake, don't you?"

Ginny squirmed. "I do now. But do you honestly think I would get involved in some silly girl's crush?"

I looked at Dave, who shrugged his shoulders. Ginny was clearly the perpetrator of these attacks, but neither of us had the remotest idea why she did it.

The Inspector leaned back against the desk and folded his arms. "Miss Whitaker, I have left the comfort of my marina-front apartment and the warm embrace of the woman I love on a cold, wet night to be here. With the Reverend's help, I have brought you for questioning with minimal fuss in order to preserve your dignity out of respect for your position in this community. So please, do not insult me by wasting anymore of my time. I know you did it. Simply tell me why."

Ginny smirked. *She's enjoying this.* Miss Whitaker believes she has won. Heavens knows what the prize is, but she's convinced it's in the bag. This woman would do anything to win. *Darcy! The stolen box. A competitive woman is not above deliberately sabotaging the opposition... Devious Doughnuts, Batman.* Like a fight scene from Adam West's television series, clues whirled into my mind with a Zammo! Thwack! POW!

I pulled a small wooden chair from the corner and dragged it over close to where the Guide mistress sat. Our knees touched. I wanted to see her reaction up close. "This isn't about Simon, is it? It's about the star. Simon just got in the way. Wrong place, wrong time. What were you trying to do? Rig the lighting to give whoever put up the star a minor shock when they crowned the tree? Or had you not thought it through that far? Perhaps you simply wanted it to short out, so the event would be an anti-climax. Embarrassing even. I mean, you weren't prepared to lose yet another year. You know Mary couldn't take that. You care a lot for your friend, don't you?

"Is it wrong to want to look after someone? I am duty-bound to protect those in my charge."

"Mary is putting on a brave face, but she is struggling with her grief and losing so much of what she loves. Her son turning his back on his father's legacy. The Brownies choosing the Cubs. Even Jake choosing Orla, or even the Fisks. His friendship with Simon. Mary is feeling very lonely, isn't she?"

"Do you have any idea what it is like to watch a good friend, your best friend, vanish before your own eyes, Reverend? But sabotage, that's a stretch even for someone of your intellect." Ginny's devotion burned into my soul.

"Ginny, you had Darcy stealing doughnuts from the rival camp. They couldn't sell products they didn't have."

The Guide leader raised her hand and rubbed away the guilt from her forehead. "You are very good at all this, aren't you? I can see why Edwina thinks you are such a good match for her Lawrence. A woman with such a mind is a thing of beauty." She sighed back into the chair. "I never met a man who could match me. Who could challenge me intellectually. But in my female friends, I've been blessed. I am surrounded by amazing talents. Yes, the Guides are for girls only. Boys undermine us. Men stifle us. They try to contain us. We have to be twice as good to receive half the recognition. We cannot allow them to win, do you see? And at baking! It's unconscionable. I cannot let it stand. I could not."

Dave stepped forward. "So, all of this. Putting an innocent man into hospital. Endangering the life of the parish priest. Everything was because you were to lose a cake competition?"

"I never meant to hurt Reverend Ward. Or that buffoon, Banks, either. I wasn't trying to hurt anyone. I merely wanted to stop the lights from working. He tried to stop me and got fried in the process. Who is stupid enough to touch a live wire?"

"But?" I was confused.

"I was wearing insulated rubber gloves. Be prepared. I am a life-long Guider. And, just for the record, I'd never go anywhere near a live wire with a metal pen knife. Swiss army or otherwise." Ginny bristled at our stupidity. "I'm sorry for what happened earlier in the church. The incident with the tree was also an accident. I saw the star at the top and guess, well, I just saw red. I unplugged the cable and used it to pull the tree down. To be honest, Reverend, I didn't even know you were there. My knife must have fallen out as I ran away. Not my finest moment I'll grant you."

Dave paced around the back of the carver chair. "So you want us to believe both occasions were accidents?"

"Inspector, you can believe what you like, but you wanted the truth, and that is it. Not very exciting, I'm afraid, but the truth very seldom is."

God Bless Us, Everyone!

Inspector Lovington sent Ginny home with a figurative slapped wrist and a time slot to attend Stourchester police station to have her statement taken. I found it oddly comforting that there was no murderous intent behind what happened. The tree and I recovered from our tussle almost injury-free, and Sam delighted me with a phone call early Christmas Eve morning to let me know that Simon Banks was awake and talking to the police.

The only other piece of breaking news was that the coroner's office had identified the body found near St Mildred's as Prudence's old friend, Janet Fairbanks. A sad, grisly discovery, but another mystery solved.

And so I sat, in the wee small hours of Christmas Eve/Day wrapping last minute presents by the fire in the morning room after a blissfully uneventful midnight mass. And when I say last minute gifts, I mean glass fish. Some may see this as a cheapskate move, others as an efficient and thrifty response to a busy diary of vicaring and sleuthing, but the truth was I loved these fish. They were representations of my former life. The life I had before I returned to Wesberrey. To the people who know me, they are as much a part of me as my brown eyes and wobbly skin. As I chose which multi-coloured beauty to give to my mother, sisters, friends, aunts, nieces, and nephew — my love for them both led my decision. I would keep a select few and display them proudly in my new home for many happy years to come.

I truly relished the serenity of my last night in the vicarage alone.

Tilly had worked in the pub till late and was staying there overnight. Phil and Barbara had invited her to join them for breakfast on Christmas morning. I understood why she accepted. For starters, she was to work their Christmas Day lunch shift, but also, I had morning mass to prepare for. My mother would arrive at the crack of stupid to cook turkey and all the trimmings for the full house of festivities planned for later in the day. A leisurely morning of warm toast and cosy slippers was not on the agenda.

Lawrence was to spend his last Christmas morning as a single man at home with his mother. Traditionally, they opened their presents together before breakfast. With my family, it was always something we did after the Queen's speech. *Now the King's speech, oh how things change?* Nothing is forever. They say the only certainties in life are change and death. My year on Wesberrey had proven that to be the case.

Mum had finished the alterations to my dress during the week and I was under strict orders not to gain a single pound before Saturday. *My feverish wrapping will burn off these chocolate liquors and tiny glass of advocaat. Curling the ribbons alone must take at least a hundred calories a pop.* My father used to make us snowball cocktails every Christmas. At 17% proof maybe it was not the wisest thing to give to children. *Hey, it was the seventies. Things were different then...*

Christmas Night will bring many familiar things back from the past. I had board games ready and we always play charades. Of course, there will be the corny jokes that fall from the Christmas crackers. Mum will have bought socks for everyone. No one will eat the Christmas pudding, and only Rosie and I will eat the sprouts. *I've always loved those mini green cabbages — don't judge me.*

Hopefully, Zuzu won't spend this year crying on the stairs over the latest man she needs out of her life yesterday — especially as Dave's going to join us. There is no Teddy to drag Rosie and Luke away early because they have a long drive home. And for the first time in decades, three generations of sisters will gather around the Yule tree and give thanks for the year's blessings and the life to come.

We will say goodbye to the year that's passed and the people we have lost along the way. Hugo and Alfie slept together in front of the glow of the fire beside me. They had lost people in their fluffy lives too. Now we had each other. I had discovered or rediscovered so much coming back to Wesberrey, and in just over twenty-four hours, I would marry my one true love, found at last.

***

The usual suspects attended morning mass. Phil and Barbara had left the 'heathen' Tilly in charge of lunch preparations. *Heathens are very useful in this modern, twenty-four-seven age.* Despite the gale force wind outside threatening to drown out our prayers, the spirit of the congregation was one of joyful celebration of our Saviour's birth.

People can, and do, argue about Christmas being a made-up religious festival that piggy-backed off the back of earlier pagan rites. That Jesus's actual birthday was most likely in the spring. Shepherds were out tending their flocks and so on. And many versions of Christianity put greater emphasis on Epiphany and/or Easter. Other world religions, naturally, don't celebrate it at all. However, I love it above all our feast days. Christmas is about coming together with the people we love to give thanks for all we have experienced and shared together. To quote crooner Andy Williams — it's the most wonderful time of the year.

I hung back to collect the stray hymnals the Scouts had missed from their swoop of the benches at the end of the mass. The promise of striped candy cane in the hall had proven a major distraction. So distracting, I had an armful of books by the time I reached the last row.

"Here, Reverend, let me help you."

"Not to worry Ernest, I've got this."

Ernest?

I turned to see my former churchwarden standing tall and looking as sparkly as a strand of tinsel.

Tom was next to him, shaking the churchwarden nomination box Barbara had placed near the back door. "Hmm, sounds like quite a few volunteers in here, but you won't be needing them, Vicar."

"Er, I won't. Why is that?"

Tom smiled at his partner, and Ernest smiled back. "We had an appointment at Stourchester General yesterday. And it's great news."

"Reverend Ward. I've been given the all clear! My cancer is in remission. It's a miracle! An actual miracle."

I do, I do, I do, I do, I do.

Rosemary hammered out the opening notes of Mendelssohn's wedding march. Family and friends filled the flower festooned pews of St Bridget's. Clouds of creamy white roses and wisps of baby's breath decorated every conceivable surface. I walked down towards the altar on my uncle Byron's arm, pinching my hand under the matching rose and gypsophila bouquet to check I wasn't dreaming.

Ahead of me stood the tall, blond, devastatingly gorgeous man who was soon to be my husband. Lawrence's best man, an old friend from university, was unable to come (well, he lived in Auckland, New Zealand and this was the day after Christmas - flights were uber expensive), so he had asked Dave to step in.

What a handsome pair they made in their navy morning suits, with long tails, grey trousers and gold brocade waistcoats. The top hats were a particularly dapper touch. *I almost feel underdressed.*

The Bishop stood equally well attired in a gold chasuble and stole. His voice sang us through the ceremony to the exchanging of vows.

"Do you, Lawrence Algernon Richard Pixley, take Jessamy Anne Ward to be your wife, to have and to hold from this day forward; for better, for worse, for richer, for poorer, in sickness and in health, to love and to cherish, till death do you part, according to God's holy law."

This is it? Say I do. Say I do.

Lawrence fixed me with his steel-blue eyes. "I do."

Thank you, lord!

I didn't hear what came next. The world around me faded away. Only Lawrence was real. I have conducted hundreds of weddings myself. It was my turn next. I knew that in a few moments, I would utter the two short words that would forever bind me to the man before me. His smile told me it was time.

"I do."

Lawrence slipped a gold band onto my finger. I took his ring from the velvet cushion the bishop was holding and returned the favour. A giggle fought its way out. Fortunately, it was contagious and seconds later, all three of us were sniffling back the laughter.

Bishop Marshall restored order by reminding us both why we were here. "Now that you both have committed yourselves to one another and to your Holy Union through the sacred vows that you have taken and by the giving and receiving of these rings, I now pronounce you husband and wife. Those whom God has joined together may He generously bless Forever. You may now kiss the bride."

Lawrence puckered his lips, still fighting back the titters, and bowed his head towards mine. His lips, soft and searching, found mine to be equally keen to seal the deal.

The assembled crowd cheered and Rosemary fired up the organ once more. From organ procession to organ procession, my life changed forever. I walked in a single woman. Now I am skipping outside with my husband's arm intertwined with mine.

The parish pixies, a.k.a. my sisters, mother, aunts, and nieces, had been decorating the church hall all morning. They forbade me from taking a sneaky peek, so the sight that greeted me as we opened the entrance doors stopped me in my tracks. White linen cloths covered the guest's tables, each in turn covered in white crockery with gilt edges. Sparkly crystal glassware twinkled with fairy lights. There were white rose centrepieces on every table and the wooden chairs sported more sprigs of gypsophila. From the central ceiling beam hung a huge rotating Mirrorball, that caught the light from two rows of spotlights as it turned, reflecting golden stars from floor to ceiling. Each place setting had a white Christmas cracker with the guest's name handwritten in black ink on the barrel. A tall white artificial pine tree stood in the corner, covered in lights and gold ornaments. *I detect a white and gold theme.*

I squeezed my husband's hand and squealed. "It's perfect!"

"No," he replied. "You are."

Oh, yes, I could get very used to this.

The catering manager introduced herself and went through the menu with us. With a nod to the gathering crowd outside, she left us to greet our guests. One by one, we shook hands with family and friends. Though Mum tried to hide it, I knew she had been crying. Lawrence's mother's eyes were red-rimmed too. They walked together to the top table, consoling each other on their loss — and their gain.

Other guests streamed past us to take their seats. It was wonderful to see so many cheerful faces all dressed in their occasion best. All my friends from Wesberrey were there, except for Lady Arabella, who had sent her apologies. It transpired she and Hugh Burton had wedding plans of their own and were too busy sunning themselves on their honeymoon in the Algarve to join us.

My sisters and nieces, as always, looked sensational. Close behind, Dave, Dominic and Bob McGuire had formed an unlikely alliance and rolled in, joking around and faux-punching each other in the guts. Tilly, Luke and Byron were so keen to sit down and eat they almost skipped straight past us. Sam, Leo, and Martha came in next, chatting amongst themselves about something so important they only stopped their conversation to congratulate us before resuming where they left off. Karen sped by too, but I pulled her back and apologised for avoiding her.

"I understand." She faltered. Tears formed, but she shook them away. "You are building a new life here. You don't need to be around death and misery. And you're right. Ellen would want me to move on, too. I've found myself a job. Just a few hours a week. But it's a start. We'll meet up for brunch perhaps, in the new year."

"Yes, start off the new year with a bang!"

The line continued. Tom and Ernest simply beamed. Audrey and Stanley Matthews appeared truly honoured to be invited. Avril and Verity wearing matching dresses, sighed in unison when Lawrence told them he had no bachelor friends he could introduce them to, leaving Phil, Rosemary and Barbara to bring up the rear. Only my aunts were still waiting outside.

They were talking to a young woman dressed in a petrol-blue coat, her hair in a high ponytail. She had her back to me, but there was something about her that was very familiar.

Cindy broke from the group and called me over. "Jess, darling, you look divine. Such a beautiful ceremony, truly wonderful. I have a little surprise for you. Come." She patted my new husband on the arm. "Lawrence, sweetie, do you mind if I borrow your wife for a second?"

Not waiting for him to reply, Cindy whisked me off to join her sister.

My Aunt Pamela waved her hand at their companion. "Jess, I would introduce you, but I believe you have met."

The blue coat turned. It was Tabitha Wells, the parapsychology student from Stourchester University.

"Er, welcome, Tabitha. This is a surprise. Please join us. I'm sure we can find a spare chair and there will be more than enough food."

"But I already have an invitation." She held up an embossed card. I recognised it at once. The name on the card was Muriel's.

"I don't understand." But I did. I understood exactly who was standing before me. "Muriel?"

"Yes, it's me, Vicar. You need to get back to your wedding breakfast. We can talk later. I'm afraid I will need your help, my dear."

***

Muriel and Tabitha had swapped places. How I could help was a mystery that would have to wait for another day. This was my wedding day.

Luke had fixed up an impressive PA system and was playing a selection of great love songs from the past five decades. It proved to be the most wonderful accompaniment to the seemingly never ending food and wine.

Once dessert had been served and only the cheese board remained, it was time for our first dance.

The lights dimmed.

Lawrence led me out into the centre of the hall. Tables packed with our guests fell silent. Lawrence raised a hand to give Luke the signal and then wrapped it around my waist. "Mrs Pixley, may I have the honour of the first dance?" The soaring violins of an Etta James's classic filled the air as my husband spun me around. We came to a gentle stop. Lawrence pressed his lips to mine as the songstress serenaded us with the truest words I had ever heard. "...here we are in heaven. For you are mine... At last."

Yup, I truly love the bones of this man.

About the Author

Penelope lives on an island off the coast of Kent, England, with her four children and an elderly Jack Russell Terrier. A lover of murder mystery and cups of tea (served with a stack of digestive biscuits), she writes quaint cosy mysteries and other feel-good stories from a corner table in the vintage tea shop on the high street. Penelope loves nostalgia and all things retro. Her taste in music is also very last century.

Find out more about Penelope at www.penelopecress.com.

Free Books and More

Get sneak peaks, exclusive giveaways, behind the scenes content, and more. Plus, you'll be notified of Fan Pricing events when they occur and get exclusive offers from other authors because I have a lot of friends in the industry. More importantly, signing up to receive my newsletter means you will get a small stack of free stories.

There will be no spam, I promise, just information about me, the books, the characters, how it came about and where it is all going.

Copy this link into your browser to check it out!

https://mailchi.mp/fd47a6eb4ae5/patricialist

If you are a social media fan, you should click the link below to join my very active Facebook group. You'll find a host of friends waiting there, some of whom have been with me from the very start.

My Facebook group get first notification when I publish anything new, plus cover reveals and free short stories, but more than that, they all interact with each other, sharing inside jokes, and answering question.

Copy this link into your browser to check it out!

https://www.facebook.com/groups/1151907108277718

Want to know more?

Greenfield Press is the brainchild of bestselling author Steve Higgs. He specializes in writing fast paced adventurous mystery and urban fantasy with a humorous lilt. Having made his money publishing his own work, Steve went looking for a few 'special' authors whose work he believed in.

Georgia Wagner was the first of those, but to find out more and to be the first to hear about new releases and what is coming next, you can join the Facebook group by copying the following link into your browser - www.facebook.com/GreenfieldPress

More Books By Steve Higgs

Blue Moon Investigations
Paranormal Nonsense
The Phantom of Barker Mill
Amanda Harper Paranormal Detective
The Klowns of Kent
Dead Pirates of Cawsand
In the Doodoo With Voodoo
The Witches of East Malling
Crop Circles, Cows and Crazy Aliens
Whispers in the Rigging
Bloodlust Blonde – a short story
Paws of the Yeti
Under a Blue Moon – A Paranormal
Detective Origin Story
Night Work
Lord Hale's Monster
The Herne Bay Howlers
Undead Incorporated
The Ghoul of Christmas Past
The Sandman
Jailhouse Golem
Shadow in the Mine
Ghost Writer

Felicity Philips Investigates
To Love and to Perish
Tying the Noose
Aisle Kill Him
A Dress to Die For
Wedding Ceremony Woes

Patricia Fisher Cruise Mysteries
The Missing Sapphire of Zangrabar
The Kidnapped Bride
The Director's Cut
The Couple in Cabin 2124
Doctor Death
Murder on the Dancefloor
Mission for the Maharaja
A Sleuth and her Dachshund in Athens
The Maltese Parrot
No Place Like Home

Patricia Fisher Mystery Adventures
What Sam Knew
Solstice Goat
Recipe for Murder
A Banshee and a Bookshop
Diamonds, Dinner Jackets, and Death
Frozen Vengeance
Mug Shot
The Godmother
Murder is an Artform
Wonderful Weddings and Deadly
Divorces
Dangerous Creatures

Patricia Fisher: Ship's Detective Series
The Ship's Detective
Fitness Can Kill
Death by Pirates
First Dig Two Graves

Albert Smith Culinary Capers
Pork Pie Pandemonium
Bakewell Tart Bludgeoning
Stilton Slaughter
Bedfordshire Clanger Calamity
Death of a Yorkshire Pudding
Cumberland Sausage Shocker
Arbroath Smokie Slaying
Dundee Cake Dispatch
Lancashire Hotpot Peril
Blackpool Rock Bloodshed
Kent Coast Oyster Obliteration
Eton Mess Massacre
Cornish Pasty Conspiracy

Realm of False Gods
Untethered magic
Unleashed Magic
Early Shift
Damaged but Powerful
Demon Bound
Familiar Territory
The Armour of God
Live and Die by Magic
Terrible Secrets

Printed in Great Britain
by Amazon

20130084R00102